The
Blood King
Conspiracy
(Matt Drake #2)

David Leadbeater

ISBN: 1481980580
ISBN-13:9781481980586

Other books by David Leadbeater:

The Bones of Odin (Matt Drake #1)

Chosen

Walking with Ghosts (a short story)

Connect with the author on Twitter:

@dleadbeater2011

Visit the author's website:

www.davidleadbeaternovels.com

Follow the author's Blog

www.davidleadbeaternovels.blogspot.co.uk/

All helpful, genuine comments are welcome. I would
love to hear from you.
davidleadbeater2011@hotmail.co.uk

DEDICATION

I would like to dedicate this book to my
daughter,
Megan,

'brighter than the sun and moon. . .'

And to all the wonderful, selfless #Indie authors
who support me every day on Twitter. You
know who you are.

CHAPTER ONE

Hayden Jaye dimmed the lights as she entered her private alcove of the living room she was sharing with five lethal men.

Her laptop shone brightly, gently whirring to itself as if in anticipation of the upcoming attention.

Hopefully, so was Ben Blake.

Hayden typed in Ben's Skype address before taking a moment to scan the room. She was tired and worn. This assignment was, in the words of her boss - the Secretary of Defence - not only a career maker, but a potential career killer too. In more ways than one.

It was by far the biggest and most dangerous she had ever tackled. Her fellow CIA agent, the massive Hawaiian, Mano Kinimaka, had heard whispers the entire agency was abuzz with the implications of it.

Some agents were taking bets . . .

Hayden tapped the laptop, imagining the connection firing itself off around the globe towards the UK. She spoke to Ben every day, job permitting, and for the most part she was loving it. She found herself missing his boyish charm, his innocence. Sometimes, she even found herself thinking about him during work. But then she forced herself to stop and remember the promise she had made to her father, and considered never contacting Ben Blake again.

But, for now, the thrill drove her on.

Ben's smiling face came scarily close to the screen, his long hair whipping past. For a computer geek he really didn't get this Skype thing.

"Killed anyone today?" His grin showed he didn't get the grown-up thing either.

"There's time," Hayden said through gritted teeth, then actually found herself almost grinning back. What the hell . . .?

"So what did you do?" Ben was floundering already. To give him his due it was hard work, this digital-interaction thing. When you talked this way every night you soon ran out of things to say.

Hayden cast a glance at her five-man team busy playing poker, standing guard, and texting loved-ones. "We did ok," she said softly. "No one here knew how deep this thing went and no one knew how high the stakes were. Well, today we learned a little, and we're doing . . . ok." Learned a little? She thought. Biggest understatement since the words 'Houston, we have a problem' were uttered.

"Good. Umm . . . Matt and Kennedy say Hi. How's Miami?"

"Excellent," Hayden rubbed her forehead tiredly. "Say it back for me. And Miami's Miami. Doesn't change a lot."

"Cool. Hey, you ok?"

"I guess so. Jonathan's having a tough time up on the Hill. He's fighting budget cuts versus young marine's lives. That sort of thing."

"The Wall of Sleep are, at the time of talking, number 96 on the Indie chart."

Hayden didn't miss the self-indulgent change of subject. "If only we could all have earned our fame from a single incident," she said, then kicked herself. Ben's band had earned itself a name and a record deal directly because of his involvement in what everyone now referred to as the 'Odin thing'.

And, truth be told, he deserved it.

"Sorry, man, it's tense down here."

"No worries, Hay. I miss you."

Hayden was about to reply, her demeanour softening, when her number two in the team, Kinimaka, hissed a warning at them all. It was the code-word for 'be alert, unknown contact.' Now Kinimaka was known and teased as the loveable giant, the not-too-bright muscle of their crack team, but when Mano Kinimaka issued a warning, you shot to attention.

Hayden left Ben talking to air, instantly alert, and glided towards the centre of the room. All eyes were on Kinimaka who was scrutinizing the security system that guarded the Miami-based CIA safe-house.

"Shadows," he was saying, his voice thick with a strong Hawaiian accent. "Clever shadows," he turned a steely gaze on them. "I don't like the look of this."

Hayden's mind was calm. Clever shadows. The people out there were specialists. She motioned quickly to the others in her team - Wyatt Godwin, Bowers, Mawby and Carrick.

"Getcha positions, guys. Move."

She picked up a rectangular receiver that lay like an ant crawling on a mountain against Kinimaka's trunk-like arm, and punched the button. Resounding thumps sounded out as unseen deadlocks bolted, and shutters fastened together.

The receiver also acted as a panic button. The CIA were already mobilising.

"Eight minutes, max," Hayden said as reassuringly as she could. She cast another glance over Kinimaka's shoulder.

Nothing moved out there. The Hawaiian screwed his face up and sent a confused shrug at her. "Maybe-"

In the next dreadful moment Hayden heard a sound she could hardly comprehend. The staccato pounding of all the locks being clicked back. The clunk of the shutters opening.

But she held the only remote, and the codes were known to only a few at Langley . . .

Mayhem scattered her thoughts. Men with masks and bodysuits came flooding fluidly through the door. Another loud noise and she knew the rear door had been blown in. Within ten seconds one of the best CIA teams in the U.S. was stunned and floundering.

But they were not lost.

Mano Kinimaka bellowed, picked up the surveillance table, and threw it overhand at the invaders. Wires, consoles and router boxes clattered to the floor and smashed against the walls as the massive object arced through the air before crashing into and taking down half a dozen men. Grunts and cries rent the air.

Kinimaka leapt towards them.

Hayden rolled as the gunfire started. Masked men came at her from three sides. She came up hard and clunked one in the face with her gun, side-stepped another, and shot the third point blank. He crumpled instantly, blood painting the air where his body had stood a second before.

Noisy hell surrounded her.

Men yelling. Guns exploding. Bullets ricocheting and tearing apart everything they encountered. Kinimaka had launched his bulk towards the door, seemingly in an attempt to block it, but the enemy kept pushing in. Jeez, how many of these bastards were there?

Three of them hit Kinimaka hard. The loveable giant crumpled. Hayden felt a three-pronged jolt of fear and hate and adrenalin. If they hurt Mano, they would pay. She bounded over a still-writhing body, shooting two bullets into the legs of the man closest to her. She peeled him off Kinimaka and threw his bulk aside, then levelled her pistol at the next guy's forehead.

Knowing she couldn't wait she pulled the trigger. Blood, brain matter and bone exploded and blew back in her face. She snarled. Kinimaka had the third guy by the neck, a big man but just a scrawny chicken in the Hawaiian's hands. The guy's eyes bulged like giant marbles. Kinimaka shook him until his neck broke and threw him to the floor.

Six more masked men squeezed through the door. Hayden fired until her clip was empty. She heard her team backing her up. Bullets whizzed by, and she heard the terrible screams of her colleagues behind her.

More enemy figures pushed in from the back door. Guns bristled in more hands than she could count. The heavy atmosphere in the room suddenly became overwhelming, as thick as liquefied guilt, and the CIA agents began to see that they had been outnumbered and out-thought.

Hayden slowly lowered her weapon. She sensed more than saw Kinimaka as he stood down for a moment, but knew he was coiled and ready for the next order.

There was an abrupt lull. The sound of war still roared in their ears as the room grew strangely still. Profound tension passed from eye to eye, as quick and as weighty as death and ruin.

A man with short hair and chiselled features walked into view, pushing his way to the front of the veritable crowd of bad guys. Hayden counted fifteen standing, seven on the floor. Good enough on a normal day, but this . . . this was crazy.

"I guess you're the girl," the lead man spoke with an American southern accent and motioned to his men. They stepped forward, took Hayden's gun and roughly bound her wrists with plastic ties. The lead CIA agent didn't panic; she still had nightmares about her treatment at the hands of the German, Abel Frey, and in particular, that psycho-bitch Alicia Myles. Hayden kept her focus and remembered her training.

The lead man spoke again. "And we need two more." He pointed to Kinimaka and one of the agents behind her. "That big bastard we can torture for longer," he said, his lips curling in a sneer. "And him, he's the last one standing."

Hayden whipped her head round and tried to hold in a gasp. Wyatt Godwin stood swaying in position. The other three agents, Bowers, Mawby and Carrick lay prone on the floor, writhing, gasping, having taken bullets.

Men pushed past her and bound Godwin's hands before shoving him to the ground next to Kinimaka. She saw the men trying to bind the big Hawaiian's wrists with plastic ties, trying hard to hide the fact that they wouldn't reach all the way around.

Lead man saw it anyway, eagle eyes everywhere. "Fools. Just keep your guns on the big bastard. If he looks dangerous treat him like a rhino. Shoot the kneecaps." The warped grin showed how amusing he thought he was.

But even in his sleep Mano Kinimaka looked dangerous. His guards glanced at each other with worried looks.

Now lead man finally turned his eyes towards Hayden. "We don't have a lot of time, I know that. So you'll hear it straight. That's my promise. You will all die. Eventually. These three," he motioned towards Bowers, Mawby and Carrick with his big Desert Eagle, "are dead already." A slimy tongue flashed across dry lips. "You three have a choice. Die easy or . . ."

The man shocked her by suddenly leaping in her face and grabbing her throat in a steel-fingered choke hold. Almost immediately she saw stars, and her legs threatened to give way. But even that wasn't enough. The man buried his fist into her stomach, grinning as he struck once, twice, three times, and all the while his fingers tightened.

"Name's Boudreau," he whispered. "Pleased to make your acquaintance, Hayden Jaye."

He walked away, letting her slither to the ground just for show. Hayden lay there a minute, trying to breathe.

Boudreau came back and stuck a boot before her blurry eyes. "What was I saying? Oh, yeah, die easy . . . or die screaming, bitches. Your call."

Hayden began to gain some focus and managed to sit up. She saw that Boudreau's men had already dragged Bowers to his feet. The tall, good-looking father of two was white with fear and pain, gasping so hard his sides were heaving. Blood soaked through the side of his jacket.

"I doubt you'll talk," Boudreau addressed his comment to Hayden. "So this one's for the fun of it all."

The leader walked over to Bowers, took out a wicked blade, and cut the agent's throat before anyone could react. Even then the wickedness employed by their captors wasn't over. The men holding him deliberately kept him upright and walked him around as his throat sprayed red mist everywhere. Walls. Carpet. Windows. It was a mercy when Bowers finally crumpled and they let him fall to the floor.

Boudreau raised his eyebrows towards Hayden.

"Like that? He's next." The blade levelled at Mawby, short and stocky and due to be married in eight weeks.

Hayden played for time. "You haven't even asked a question, for Christ's sake. What do you want, Boudreau?"

"Not to be played for a fool, Miss Jaye. You see, my boss is, quite possibly the craziest, most dangerous man in the world. And he's asked me to get answers. So-"

Quickly, Boudreau spun on the spot and threw his knife. It slammed through Mawby's throat. The agent would have staggered back into the wall if it weren't for the men holding him. They wasted no time parading him up and down. Hayden turned away from the bloody spectacle, sickened.

Boudreau said his boss was the craziest? The guy was registering high up the whacko-meter himself.

"And so we come to the last," Boudreau had retrieved his knife and was now winking at Carrick. "Where d'ya want it, son? C'mon. Where?"

Hayden snapped. "What the hell do you want, Boudreau? Our investigation? Details?"

"Now you're talking."

Hayden was counting down. Help couldn't be more than three minutes away.

"The Blood King," she said cryptically. "We've heard about some guy called the Blood King today."

"You've heard of him!" Boudreau's eyes practically bulged. "Heard! Love of God, no wonder he wants an example made of you all, CIA or not."

Another minute ticked by.

Hayden said: "Not just the CIA, Boudreau. The American government."

The southerner's eyes widened a little and for a moment Hayden thought the crazy, hard-man betrayed a glimmer of fear. "Nothing," he breathed. "Even that is nothing to the Blood King."

He spun away and strode over to Carrick. The agent stood half-bowed, blood already leaking from a thigh wound, but his eyes betrayed nothing as he stared the evil man with the knife right in the eyes.

"Good," Boudreau drawled. "I almost feel a pride in you. Almost-" The knife flashed.

"We know someone's found the answer . . ." Hayden cried, desperate and sweating and shaking with emotion. " . . . to the Bermuda Triangle! We know, you evil bastard."

Boudreau shot her a smug, evil leer and then deliberately turned and slowly pushed his bloody blade through Carrick's neck until it emerged the other side. The strength of the man was shocking.

Carrick slumped. Boudreau left the knife where it was and signalled his men. "Double-time. The cavalry's coming," he winked in Hayden's direction. "Don't fret, dear. Those three got off easy compared to what's gonna happen to you."

David Leadbeater

After they vacated the house the only sound that remained was the slow drip of blood and the gentle whirring of the laptop.

CHAPTER TWO

Ben Blake sat staring at the dark computer screen for a few moments, then started screaming. Within seconds Drake and Kennedy were at the door.

"What the hell are you pissing about at, Blakey?" Drake was carrying a tea towel, a somewhat strange look for the ex-soldier. "Nappy rash playing you up again?"

Kennedy was smiling. "Maybe the Backstreet Boys are getting back together? Again?"

"H . . . Hayden. She, . . . " Ben's felt a heavy pounding in his head, as if a demon was trying to smash its way through his skull, " . . . something just ha . . . happened."

Drake realised his best friend was terrified. "Hey! Hey, mate, calm down. Just sit back for a sec. It'll be alright. Breathe."

Ben took a moment to gather his nerves. "I was just talking to her. Hayden. I think . . . I think they got ambushed, or invaded, or whatever. There was fighting." Ben's voice fell. "Gunshots."

"No way." Drake twisted his head to take in the computer screen. It offered nothing but an empty wall that sported a colour so drab and life-sucking it could have been used to decorate a tax office.

"I can't hear anything," Drake said. "Did you hear anything?"

"It was muffled, but I heard screaming and fighting and a few words at the end."

"Where was she?"

"Miami. At a safe-house. That's all I know. All I'm allowed to know."

Kennedy laid a hand on his shoulder. "Any ideas what she was working on?" Straight to what she thought was the heart of the matter, Drake thought.

Ben shook his head. "No idea."

They all stared at the empty screen.

Then Ben said, "The last thing I heard her say, well, scream, was we've found the secret to the Bermuda Triangle."

Kennedy took a deep breath.

Drake didn't move for a moment, and then closed his eyes. Here we go again.

*****

Drake and Kennedy made eye contact and doubled-ribbed Ben for his increased pleasure. "Barry Manilow, eh? Didn't know you were a fan, Blakey?"

"Worst song of all time?" Kennedy bobbed her head with mock-seriousness. "I think so."

Drake snapped his fingers. "Maybe you could cover it on the new album?"

Ben's worried, blank face showed that he wouldn't be placated lightly.

Drake and Kennedy immediately began to make calls. Since the 'Odin thing' they both had access to some high level people, including the U.S Secretary of Defence's aide, a weedy, geeky guy who always ran around with a briefcase that practically dwarfed him.

As the phones rang and buzzed and lost signal they met each other's eyes. Kennedy had been living with Drake for six weeks now, ever since the demise of Abel Frey. She had taken an extended vacation from the NYPD with a view to never going back. The couple were warily enjoying their time together, careful not to push the wrong buttons or scratch at any raw wounds.

For now, none of them needed to work. There had been some quiet remuneration after they helped save the world. Ben was even looking at moving out and renting his own place, especially since his band, the Wall of Sleep, had picked up a recording contract on the back of his Odinic success; a development that held much juicy mileage for Matt and Kennedy.

Drake got hold of Wells immediately. "Hey."

"You again."

"Missed me?"

"Only in the field."

Drake paused. "I guess we never did get that Mai time, eh mate?"

"I'm used to being let down, Drake . . . by you."

"Christ! Don't be a pansy, Wells. Something big has come up."

"It might. If I got me some Mai time."

"Listen. It looks like a crack CIA team were . . ." Drake hesitated to repeat anything final. "hit today. In Miami. It happened a few minutes ago and I need details, Wells. Real fast."

The SAS Commander seemed to take an interest. "Really? OK, mate, I'll make a call."

Drake was about to hit another number when Ben shouted again. He raced back into his lodger's room, Kennedy a step behind.

"Someone just burst in," the young man was pointing at a black screen. "I heard voices, shouting. I heard real shock, Matt, as if someone got the shit scared out of them. Someone swore, and then I think the laptop was slammed shut."

"Can you Skype it?" Kennedy asked. "You know. Make it ring again."

Ben clicked a few buttons. Nothing happened. "The connection must have gone down."

Kennedy shook her head. "All we friggin' need. Wait . . . Hi, is that Justin?"

The Secretary of Defence's aide was called Justin Harrison.

Kennedy affirmed it was and hit him with the news. To the guy's credit if he worked as fast as he walked they'd have answers in about five minutes.

Drake sidled quietly out of the room and tried one last number. The phone was answered on the first ring.

"Long time, my friend. Long, long time." The voice that whispered in his ear was a memory of former, delicious days, sorely missed and revered.

"Well, I thought I had retired." Unconsciously he tried to clean his Yorkshire twang up to suit her cultured tones.

"It will never end, Matt Drake. You should know that. It never ends for people like you and me."

"I know you're in Florida."

"Hmm. How do you know that?"

"I still have friends in the loop." He tried to not to sound too defensive.

"I'm sure. Is Mr Wells now a stalker as well as a pervert?"

Drake winced. "To be honest, he's always been a bit of both."

"Of course. Well, what do you need?"

"It sounds stupid now. But have you . . ." he shook his head in embarrassment. " . . . heard anything about the bloody Bermuda Triangle!"

Her laugh was like the barely remembered sound of summer rain to his ears. God, he missed that sound. "I know the operation you are talking about. I know some things but not enough. Let me give you a call back."

"Brilliant." He listened as she closed the connection. He closed his eyes, remembering. After a few seconds he heard a sound from behind and whirled to look.

Kennedy stood in the doorway, staring. "Who was that?"

"Old contact." Drake collected himself and strode past her towards Ben's room. "What do we have?"

Ben's eyes were watery. He shrugged. "I don't know. Nothing, I guess."

It was Kennedy's mobile that rang first, a tune by The Pretty Reckless that shattered an uncomfortable stillness. She answered and punched the speaker button.

"It's Justin Harrison."

"I know," Kennedy drawled, still showing her cops' abruptness. "What have you got?"

"Bad news I'm afraid, Miss Moore. The CIA are still gathering information, but it seems one of their high-security Miami safe-houses was literally taken out. Quite a mess down there. Reports of some very bad deaths. Terrible stuff, Miss Moore."

Kennedy's eyes filled with tears. Drake felt his own throat choke up. "Hayden? Hayden Jaye? Is she-?"

"Well, like I said, they are still gathering but it seems three agents are missing. Possibly taken captive or . . . well, who knows? Names are Jaye, Kinimaka, and Godwin."

Drake felt his hands clench into fists at the careless use of Harrison's rhetoric. Names are . .

"She's missing? Hayden is missing?"

Ben was on his feet, trying and failing to keep his emotions in check.

Drake looked at Kennedy as she cut off the connection. "Fancy a trip to the homeland, love?"

CHAPTER THREE

Deep inside the Florida Everglades, Hayden Jaye twisted on the concrete floor. Her hands were still bound but she used Mano Kinimaka as a fulcrum and pushed to her feet.

She looked around.

They had been thrown into a makeshift cell. The place they were in was a ramshackle mess; nothing more than a few old buildings knocked together. Obviously a temporary base, but for how long? Their cell was full of empty, torn-apart cardboard boxes. Wyatt Godwin, the only other surviving member of her team, sat propped in a corner and gave her a weak smile.

Beyond a row of heavy, black bars lay a vast, untidy room, dominated by a chaos of technological clutter and weaponry that had clearly just been thrown together. Hayden counted dozens of men making their way among the jumbled islands; none wore masks.

She turned to Kinimaka. "Any ideas?"

The giant shrugged, displacing dust from his shoulders in a mushroom cloud. "Everglades. Trees. Water. Gators. The four airboats we all arrived on."

It had taken four airboats to carry the members of their enemy squad. When they arrived at their destination Hayden had seen nothing but derelict walls and overgrown doorways, but inside, the place was a veritable, if untidy, shopping mall of advanced machinery.

Hayden stared at Kinimaka. "Airboats." She repeated. He nodded.

The bars rattled. Hayden spun to see the devil responsible for the murder of three CIA agents pressing a leering face between the narrow gaps. "Ed Boudreau," he thrust a gloved hand through and made a play of shaking thin air. "Pleased to kill you."

"Likewise," Hayden whispered, knowing she shouldn't but unable to stop herself. Her father had been better than that, had taught her better than that.

"You look quite a mess, my dear," Boudreau said. "Oh, my, is that brain in your hair? Who'd have thought an enemy agent would actually have one and then lose it, eh?"

Kinimaka used the wall to stand up behind her. She didn't see him, she felt the rumbling and the shaking.

"Hey, hey big boy," Boudreau laughed. "Calm down. I'm not going to start with either of you two." His gaze fell upon Wyatt Godwin. "Hi there."

"So what do you want?" Hayden continued to evaluate their surroundings, as she knew the other two were doing.

"You touched on the subject briefly, remember? Back when your friends were painting the walls? It's a local phenomenon known as the Bermuda Triangle. Been around a few years. Tell me what you know."

"Alright, alright," said Hayden looking away. "It's a song by Barry Manilow. Early '80's, I'm guessing. Did we win?"

"He did." Boudreau motioned at Godwin. Guards appeared, levelling lethal-looking weapons at Kinimaka and her. "Don't move."

Hayden sucked in her lips. They were dead anyway. Why not try their luck now, when there were three of them? Why wait?

Survive as long as you can. The old Jaye creed had been all but branded into her. One minute, to the next, to the next. Don't provoke. Every next moment might bring you the chance you need.

Godwin struggled hard, giving one guard a bloody nose, but he was no match for three. They manhandled him out of the cell and threw him to the ground before Boudreau. "Nothing fancy," the leader said, taking out his field knife. "Tell me what you know, and it's quick. Dick me about and it's choppy choppy time." His grin left no doubt in Hayden's mind which scenario he favoured.

"Listen!" She hoped the desperation didn't show too much in her voice. She couldn't bear to watch another member of her team murdered before her eyes. Commonsense and training urged her to shut the hell up. Heart and mind said otherwise.

"We don't know much. What we learned, well, we only learned yesterday." Was it really only yesterday that her team had been laughing, excited, looking forward to their futures? Was it really only yesterday that she'd been talking to Ben Blake and torn between two minds about what to do with him?

"It's something to do with the Queen Anne's Revenge," Hayden blurted. "You know, Blackbeard's ship?"

If her father could see her now . . .

"The pirate?" Boudreau smiled condescendingly.

"Yes! They found it in '96 off the North Carolina shore and have been excavating and salvaging it ever since. And, well, pirates . . . well they tend to hoard a lot of . . . umm . . . treasure."

Surprisingly Boudreau wasn't laughing, only appraising. "You'll be telling me the Bermuda Triangle is naught but pirate booty next! Aarghh!"

With the last exclamation Boudreau sank his knife to the hilt into Godwin's thigh. The shock was so sudden that even Godwin just stared for a second. Then Boudreau twisted the hilt and ripped the blade back and Godwin started to twist and scream. Blood pooled rapidly through his trousers and across the floor.

"Anything else?"

Hayden stayed quiet.

"Tell me about the Blood King?" Boudreau all but bellowed. "Tell me about the Blood King!"

Hayden stepped back despite herself. Boudreau had gone red in the face and was sending spittle flying in her direction. Christ, even the very mention of the Blood King sent this American bad-ass into seizures.

How could that be?

"We know nothing, Boudreau. Beyond his name, and that he is looking for the item we confiscated from the Queen Anne's Revenge. That's it."

She turned a regretful gaze towards Godwin. The man's eyes had rolled up into his head. A guard was kicking him, another stabbing him. Inside five minutes one more CIA agent lay still and bleeding at Boudreau's sin-stained hands.

Hayden met the eyes of Mano Kinimaka. It was a look of finality and goodbye. A look that said 'don't judge me on how I die, judge me on how I've lived.'

Kinimaka's heavy brows raised in an open expression of sorrow. The Hawaiian was a very open man, not used to concealing his feelings.

Boudreau was already at the cage and tapping the bars with his knife, sending rivulets of blood spattering across the floor.

"You ready?" He grinned at Hayden.

Then someone shouted, a scared holler that seemed completely out of place coming from the rough brawler who stood clutching a sat-phone.

"Boudreau!"

The leader's face showed anger. "What?"

"It's him! It's him!" The phone was being brandished as if it were ablaze.

Hayden watched closely as Boudreau's face adjusted instantly from confident fury to abject terror.

Instantly.

Hayden stared in utter amazement. Whoever was on the end of that sat-phone had one of the scariest and most capable enemies she had ever known almost pissing his pants in fear.

It beggared the obvious question – who?

The Blood King?

Hayden sank back against the far wall, grateful for the respite and for the various trackers that some geek had sewn into her clothing a couple of weeks ago.

CHAPTER FOUR

As soon as the plane landed at Miami International, Drake, Ben and Kennedy were up and out of their seats with the masses, waiting to disembark. The journey had been long and strained, not helped by the fact that they had been unable to glean any more useful information. Drake was hopeful that as soon as he hit U.S. soil his previous phone calls might bear fruit. He had a nasty suspicion that Justin Harrison might not provide them with as much help as he was promising.

Through customs and past the carousels they went, on edge every step of the way. Into the bustle of the airport and scanning the crowds. Ben saw the man first.

'Drake party!' his card yelled in big, black letters.

The three of them hurried over, Drake worrying about how to keep his best friend's spirits up. Banter was pretty much out of the question. Support was always good, but the lack of news and contact was making them all fretful.

Their chauffeur drove in silence, taking them through Miami and across one of its sweeping bridges that led to the beach, and pulled up outside a big white hotel called the Fontainbleu. Drake pinched his nose as they drove, partly to alleviate the tension and the tiredness, but also to pause and come to terms with the utter vastness of this city compared to the one they had left behind.

He took the quiet time to run a few things over in his head. The past six weeks, since the end of the

'Odin thing', had been quite a ride. Kennedy and he had developed feelings for each other, but both knew they were skirting around the more profound problems in their lives - his wife, Alyson's terrible car crash and the memories of his days in the SRT, and Kennedy's dreadful memories of Thomas Kaleb, both before and during the arena battle.

And again he had been trying to get the soldier out of his head, stubborn in the belief that he would never need that part of him again.

It never ends, Matt Drake. It never ends for people like you and me.

He still had feelings for her. Mai. And right now he was closer to her than he'd been for many years. He wondered if their paths would cross.

Within minutes they were being shown to their rooms. Drake stayed True Brit and forgot to tip. Ben walked over to the room's oak-stained desk and plonked himself down.

The kid looked around. "Laptop?"

Drake felt a bit of deja vu left over from the Odin adventure, but gave him the big Sony without comment. He walked over to the rectangular windows and stared at the hotel opposite before turning his glance down the long straight road known as Collins Avenue.

The sudden silence was oppressive. Energy gnawed at him, a caged lion desperate for release. To hell with the mirror-clear, blue-and-green patchwork ocean; to hell with the bikini babes and Miami Beach.

What they needed now was information about Hayden and her team.

Kennedy stared at him from across the room. "You thinking what I'm thinking?"

"Hope not. Cos that'd make you a lesbian."

"Quit it for a second, soldier boy. You know what I mean."

"We're being compartmentalised. Kept out of the loop. They don't want us here, and they don't want us interfering."

"Like we interfered with Abel Frey." Ben mumbled.

"Governments don't think that far back," said Drake walking over to his friend. "Or forward for that matter."

Ben had typed 'Bermuda Triangle' into his laptop and was studying the returns. "Plenty here. Flight 19 was the first loss in the '50s. Woah! Listen to this, the flight leader was heard to say- 'We are entering white water, nothing seems right. We don't know where we are, the water is green, no white.' His last words. It's claimed that, ever since, there has been an unknown pattern of random, supernatural events in the region."

"And who knows, maybe before," said Kennedy shrugging.

Drake grunted. "There's nothing supernatural about it. I bet, if you check, random events happen all over the ocean. The Bermuda Triangle's just got a better PR team."

At that moment there was a knock at the door. Drake scooted over and Kennedy pulled Ben over to the curtains, partially hiding him. Drake didn't peer through the keyhole, instead he shouted in broad Yorkshire. "Who's there?"

"Justin Harrison," an impatient voice answered. "Open up!"

Drake did as requested. Jonathan Gates' secretary minced in through at the speed of sound, huge briefcase slamming around his legs. The guy must end up bruised all over by the end of that day and probably wondered where the hell he got half of them.

Ben met him head on. "Where is she?"

"We've found them. Well, we've found the general area using trackers. Then they stopped working. But we know within a few miles' radius." Like bullets, Harrison's words ripped through the air at the speed of light. "Teams are being prepped. They're going in."

Ben thought about all that. Drake tapped the aid on the shoulder. "You're sending in teams to rescue her. Just like that?"

"Yes. Very important we get her back. Huge case. Just huge. Might be the CIA's biggest case ever. She - Hayden - has information. Also, we think two other agents might be alive. Massive Mano and Godwin."

"What case?" Ben was asking as Drake evaluated his next move. Time was key here.

"The Blood King. Some huge underworld figure everyone thought was a goddamn myth. Turns out, he's real. He's tied to Blackbeard's ship and the salvage operation through the object we found."

"The one that explains the Bermuda-"

Drake shouted. "Let's go hitch a ride!"

Before even Justin Harrison could utter another word they were racing down the corridor.

*****

Drake hit speed-dial in mid-flight and got hold of Wells. "There's at least one Delta Force or SEAL team mobilising right now for an operation in the Florida Everglades. We need to be on that flight."

He snapped shut before Wells could speak. The lift plummeted at high speed. "Hope they're inbound from Miami," he said and shrugged. Time would tell.

Outside they flagged a cab and told it to head for the nearest Helipad.

"Ocean Beach or the Dade county airport?" the lazy drawl came back.

"Dade county," Drake urged and the cab shot off.

Busy roads and busy shops surrounded them. Palm trees swayed this way and that as if leaning into a lovers' embrace. The hot glare and shimmer of the sun made him wish he'd remembered to pack a pair of sunglasses. Just one pair. Sherlock, he wasn't.

Within ten minutes his mobile belted out an old Dinorock tune. "Wells?"

"A private helipad on the Rickenbacker Causeway. Signs say it's an animal sanctuary or something. It is, but it's owned by the government. Get me?"

"Got you. Speak soon."

Drake relayed their new destination to the taxi driver who grunted and shook his head. The word tourists probably crossed his lips. Drake's mobile rang again.

"Yes?" He answered shortly without thinking.

"Be nice, my friend, you might like what I have to offer."

The cultured tones again made him boomerang back in time. "Oh, it's you."

"Well, you actually sound disappointed."

"Listen, I can't speak right now." Drake was uncomfortably aware of the cab's close confines. "Call you back later." He jabbed at the disconnect button, inwardly disgusted with himself.

Kennedy was giving him the eye. "What gives, Matt?"

"Nothing. We're here." Drake hardened his thoughts and flexed his muscles. When the causeway came into view and the cab stopped Drake only had to give their names.

One of the SEAL team commanders came over to him personally. "Good to have you with us, Drake. Everyone knows what you did in Iceland. You're welcome, but . . . " his dubious gaze swivelled to include Ben and Kennedy.

"Same crew who fucked Abel Frey," Drake told him.

The SEAL-team commander nodded in respect. "Then we're ready."

It was almost time for war.

CHAPTER FIVE

Hayden found herself with a little time on her hands. Ed Boudreau had become absorbed with his boss as he tried to resolve several problems. Hayden again found herself amazed at the subservient tone this madman employed when dealing with his superior. Could anyone really be that scary?

Sprawled and broken before her cell lay Wyatt Godwin. Father of three. Surfer. Regular at the Cheesecake Factory over at Coconut Grove. Husband.

Hayden looked away before raw emotion stalled her brain. Kinimaka was staring at her.

"This Blood King," the big Hawaiian rumbled. "He don't seem all that mythical to me."

"If that's him," Hayden motioned with her head, "on the phone. I'm thinking I really don't wanna meet him."

"Tough dude, that Boudreau," Kinimaka smiled wistfully. "Not too tough though. His fear - it will undo him."

Hayden started at her colleague, not normally known for his poetic outbursts. "Is that a Hawaiian proverb, or something?"

Kinimaka laughed like a whale snoring. "Just because I'm a native and follow the traditional ways doesn't mean I quote scripture, Hayden. What I mean is, it will make him careless by dividing his attentions. That will give us our chance."

"I hope so. You know, all this could have been averted if the damn device hadn't been hauled up from Blackbeard's ship on National TV. What a fiasco."

Kinimaka shrugged. "They don't know where it is. Or what it does."

Hayden stared. "I'm not so sure, Mano. Look what the maniac's done so far. Tortured and killed a CIA team. Launched a massive assault on American soil. Set up at least one high-tech HQ. This all speaks of unbelievable resources and madness. And obsession. The worst kind."

"So this is, like, the tip of the iceberg?" Kinimaka looked genuinely shocked.

"Exactly."

Hayden heard Boudreau's voice getting closer and clammed up. In another minute the man's hard, chiselled face was pressed back up against the bars. "My apologies."

"Getting your orders, hey Ed?" Hayden tried a different tactic. "Whilst pissing your pants."

Boudreau's face didn't even crack. Indeed, he appeared to agree with her. "You don't know what this guy can do. He is one motherfucking scary bastard, believe me." Then, he seemed to remember where he was and who he was speaking to.

"Get that bitch outta that cage!" The snarl was aimed at his men who leapt as if they'd been bitten by a rabid monkey. Hayden braced herself as they came at her, fighting back, but her head-butt was expected and her kicks were easily avoided. Within a minute Hayden had been dragged out of the cage and was facing Boudreau, so close she could smell the evil that clung to him like a poisoned shroud. She could smell his sweat, his lust, his veiled terror.

He was a millimetre way, the blood-crusted blade between them, touching both their faces. But Hayden clung on to sanity with one optimistic thought.

The guards had been moving so fast, and so reactively, that they hadn't locked the cage behind them. She had to hope Kinimaka had realised too and was preparing his move.

"I was told to send an overwhelming force at you, Jaye. Twenty-one men, against a crack CIA team of six. You never stood a chance."

"Maybe that also had something to do with you knowing our safe-house codes."

Boudreau shrugged. "Maybe. I was told to hammer our point across. I think I succeeded."

"That was about sending a message?" Hayden shook her head. "To the CIA? On American soil? That's not hammering a point, Boudreau, that's clinical insanity."

"Blackbeard's ship, and the device they salvaged," Boudreau whispered. "Tell me about it or we'll see how your nose looks on the floor."

Hayden swallowed silently, and then indicted the massive array of computer terminals and other hi-tech gadgets around the room. "Looks to me like you have all the resources you need."

"We do," Boudreau sighed. "We're just being thorough. You know the drill."

She did. She watched the blade as it swayed before her. Her chance was getting close, but it needed to be sheer split-second madness and dumb luck. Then Boudreau said something that almost knocked her backwards.

"You need to tell us what you know about the second device too. The controller."

Hayden's face, unfortunately, said it all.

"Nothin'." Boudreau looked satisfied. "That's all we needed."

He thrust the knife at her. Through luck or impeccable design Kinimaka chose that precise second to make his move. Roaring like a charging polar bear he smashed through the cage door into the guards stationed on the other side. Bodies flew and crashed everywhere. Bones broke and computers and metal tables smashed to the ground and into the walls. Wire and modems and half-empty cups of coffee scattered across the rough concrete floor.

Boudreau's knife flicked away from Hayden's ribs when a guard collided with him. Hayden leapt forward, bringing her forehead down hard onto the bridge of his nose and, as he fell, slid her strapped wrists along the length of his knife blade.

The plastic snapped. Her hands were free. She cast around, brain sharp, knowing that in the melee there would be more than one discarded weapon. Kinimaka was bulldozing everything in sight. Desks, garbage cans, computer geeks and mercenaries. They fled before him like debris before a mega-flood.

A light machine-gun caught her eye. She twisted away from Boudreau's sudden lunge and skidded on her knees, grabbing the weapon in mid-slide.

Turned, already firing, instinctively knowing the positions of her enemies.

The bullets struck true. A group of guards pinwheeled in all directions, spraying blood like liquid confetti through the air. Kinimaka ducked, but barged on, and now Hayden realised that he was clearing a path to the door.

The way was open!

Hayden ran, seeing daylight. Then Boudreau rose up in her path, a mountain of murderous intent and inbred evil, leering at her whilst licking the coagulated blood from his knife.

Boudreau thrust high. Hayden slid low. The blade nicked the edge of her forehead, leaving a red furrow. She was up in less than a second, firing to cover Kinimaka, firing at the other soldiers blocking their escape, wishing just one of those bullets could have been saved for Boudreau, one of the most sadistic and dangerous men she had ever met.

*****

Outside, the intense heat of the Everglades hit her. The contrast from concrete to forested greenery gave her a moment's pause. Then Kinimaka was bellowing and she saw his great bulk bent down beside an airboat.

Sensing the immediate pursuit she put her head down and flew across the ground. Bullets pinged the air and struck hard bark around her. With a desperate effort she slewed to Kinimaka's side, making the home run before the shortstop even knew she was there.

The airboat fired up. Kinimaka leapt on board and dragged her after him like a sack of meal. Her head hit the safety cage, but with nothing more than a glancing blow. Nevertheless, blood sprayed the deck of the flat-bottomed boat. Kinimaka swivelled the stick that controlled the vertical rudders and the airboat shot off, its low sides already riddled with bullets.

"Damn." Hayden saw the three airboats they had left behind. "They'll be chasing us, Mano. You ever pilot one of these things before?"

His blank look gave her a quick insight. His words "I'm Hawaiian," gave her the answer.

"Don't worry. Just stay in the middle of the channel."

The river here was wide and the banks were carpeted in short grass, with trees beyond. Kinimaka threw the airboat through curve after curve and Hayden kept an eye out for pursuit. At first she saw nothing, but after a few minutes she heard the tell-tale whine of approaching airboats.

"Step on it, Mano."

"I think all these things go the same speed, boss. But then, I guess, I ain't really too sure."

Mano, being Mano. Hayden held on tight and watched their rear. She also watched the banks for any signs of life or alternative routes. So far, nothing jumped out at her.

"They're gaining, Mano," she said tightly as the first airboat started to close behind them. "We need a Plan B."

CHAPTER SIX

Drake met the eyes of the SEAL team as they flew towards the Everglades and their final destination. He knew what lay behind those flat, appraising stares. A slab of respect, a slice of estimation, and a complex topping of unease.

They had heard he was good, probably from their own colleagues, but would he fit with them. And, in a dick-swinging contest, could they take him?

"Answer's no," he said to the youngest, the one with eager glints. "Not until at least 2020."

"I was goin' to ask ya 'bout Alicia Myles," the boy drawled with a big grin. "She really the wildcat y'all talkin' about?"

Drake took a breath. "Wouldn't know," he said diplomatically. "We lost track . . . right after she tried to kill me."

"Heard she did a pretty good job," the lad snickered. "And that you lost track as thanks for her not murderin' you."

"She's good," Drake said, refusing to be baited whilst Hayden's life hung in the balance. "And she's not been seen for a while, kid. Let's leave it at that."

The chopper now banked sharply and Drake began to see a lot of green below. Rivers and tributaries sprawled and meandered in random patterns. Flocks of birds took to the air.

The pilot looked around. "Five minutes."

Drake steeled himself. Ben, at his side, was clenching both hands into fists, his face drip white with worry. Kennedy's face was set in a stony glare, daring anyone to challenge her.

"Ready."

The chopper swooped low, aiming straight for a ramshackle hodgepodge of buildings. Rappel lines were dropped. The SEAL team slithered down with professional swiftness, all out in less than a minute. Drake and his companions waited for the chopper to land, frustrated but knowing that the team knew its business.

The chopper landed with a mini thud. Drake leapt straight out the door. Cross-winds from the rotor blades battered him. Long grass whipped at his ankles. They were met by the SEAL team leader.

"Cleared out," he said, but his eyes were dark.

"What else?" Drake clenched his teeth.

"CIA agent, dead inside."

Ben gasped.

"Godwin," the SEAL commander said, with murder in his voice. He pointed behind Drake.

"Looks like they cleared out in a hurry, most likely using airboats. They were probably chasing our men."

Drake started walking. "Let's go get 'em."

CHAPTER SEVEN

Hayden found herself flung to the deck as Kinimaka yanked the airboat's stick and swerved past a dangerous, reedy bank. She struggled to her knees, bleeding, scraped raw in more places than she could count. Her hair would never be the same. Bullets from their pursuers peppered the airboat's sides and skimmed and whined around them.

Enemy shouts and jeers carried on the wind, making her grit her teeth as she heard threats she would rather die before enduring.

She saw the channel ahead narrowing drastically. Kinimaka threaded the needle, waterspouts shooting up beside and behind the vehicle. Hayden saw big gators disturbed and twisting away in anger as they passed.

Where the hell were they going?

"Bearings?" She shouted above the harsh roar of engine, wind and weaponry.

The big Hawaiian frowned. "Eh? Nah, there'd be more of a squeal if the bearings had gone."

"I mean do we have a heading?"

"Away from those bastards!" Kinimaka jerked a thumb behind as more light machine-gun fire preceded the popping and strafing of surrounding water.

The Hawaiian made the water surge as he negotiated another chicane. The airboat clipped the head of a small island and skipped free of the water for a second before landing with a crash and powering on. Hayden and Kinimaka made big eyes at each other.

"Shit!"

Hayden determined she should stay quiet and took a fleeting look back. She had decided that, unless their pursuers got any closer, she wasn't going to waste ammo on speeding targets.

Three airboats were tailing them, packed with bad guys. Trouble was, they knew the waters. Kinimaka didn't. It was only a matter of time before one of them recognised a short cut.

Even now she could hear Boudreau's voice, manic, a banshee chasing her along the dark and bloody byways of hell.

Then Mano hit a partially submerged island. The airboat took flight, engine roaring. Water slewed from its side and rudders in white sheets. Hayden had half a second to hear cheering from behind and then the airboat struck the shallows like a pregnant hippo.

Hard.

She was instantly propelled forward and tucked

her head and limbs in as best she could. Still, when she hit the ground the jolt jarred every bone in her body.

For a moment she was stunned. Then Kinimaka splashed down beside her like Shamu and drenched her with half the local water table.

She struggled onto her knees, partially submerged. The machine-gun was nowhere to be seen. She clapped Kinimaka about the ears, knowing she could never drag him up the sloping banks. After a moment his shaggy head came up, gasping for air.

"Thank God."

Amazingly, they were both intact. The airboat was roaring crazily, lying on its side nearby and completely unusable. Hayden surveyed the reeds and the bank. Their only hope was to climb.

At that moment the three chasing airboats came into view. One of them hit the same island that fooled Kinimaka. The vehicle took off. Men and weapons flew into the air. Hayden scrambled out of the way, yelling at Kinimaka to follow. As she scooted clear she heard splashes all around her.

Machine-guns dropping. Kennedy reached for one and prepped it. Kinimaka made ready with another. Men were now dropping all around them. Splashes and grunts and the sound of breaking bones filled the air. When a man showed more signs of life than feeble movement Kinimaka fired a bullet into him.

Hayden turned and started to scramble through the shallow water. She sloshed among the weeds, tramping desperately upwards towards the drier bank. At that moment there was a huge eruption of water and one of Boudreau's men rose up before her. His small revolver was levelled between her eyes and his twisted smile showed he had gotten lucky with the crash and decided to lie in wait.

Time stopped.

Kaleidoscopic images of stolen moments and regrets flashed through her brain: an old picture reel of a life of never-ending experiences. The man's finger tightened on the trigger . . . Kinimaka was a world away, and screaming in frustration . . .when the fifteen-foot-long gator struck the man mid-torso.

His scream was high and insanely comical. His gun spiralled away. The man disappeared in less time than it takes to blink, leaving behind him the ghost of a scream and only a hint of spilled blood.

Nothing compared to the nightmare he was now enduring as he was dragged to the bottom of the river.

Violence saturated the air.

Hayden brought every ounce of her will to bear and collected herself. It took every memory of every good thing her father had taught her. Every hard lesson and proud moment. She focused on the moment when she learned of his death, his cold murder, and remembered the life changing vows she had made right then and there.

It was all she had to spur herself on, to forget the carnage and advance. One step at a time. She reached the bank. She dug her fingers into the earth and pulled. She climbed. Then her stomach clutched with dread as she heard another enormous detonation of water behind her and out of her peripheral vision saw the nightmarish shape of the gator as it twisted and lunged for her.

In that moment of utter hell she witnessed a massive blur shooting past. It was Mano Kinimaka, roaring like a man possessed and tackling the gator around the exposed belly with a crunch they probably heard in Disneyland. The gator, no doubt in shock at being tackled by anything, let alone this man-mountain, was tipped over and thrown, back-first, into the shallows. Kinimaka landed atop it, arms encircling its body, gripping tight as if his life and the life of his boss depended on it.

And now, as Hayden balanced and rose to her feet, the men from the other two airboats began to open fire. Bullets thwacked and thudded the greenery around her, and kicked up sprays of water. Kinimaka thrashed with the gator. Hayden fell back against the muddy bank, exposed.

Brought her machine-gun around and opened fire.

And that was their last stand. Hayden, half buried in mud and muck and dripping wet, firing from the hip and felling the bad guys with every bullet. Kinimaka subduing the gator that writhed at her feet, screaming with the effort it took to hold on, eyes wild as he searched for a way to let go in relative safety.

The bad guys were advancing slowly. Boudreau was partially hidden behind his men, alternately shouting instructions and then laughing maniacally when a man right in front of him pirouetted bloodily and fell off the boat.

At that moment there was a scrambling sound behind her. Before she could turn, someone encircled her throat with a grip of iron. A cheer went up from the airboats. Hayden felt herself hauled to her feet.

The man's grip was death. Kinimaka was in dire straits below. He saw what was happening but daren't loosen his grip. Hayden fired down and back, turned the man's foot to bloody mush. He fell away, screaming soundlessly. Hayden turned and fired a burst through his chest.

Then, under fire and dead on her feet, she dragged the dead man down into the churning shallows.

"Do it!" She screamed at Kinimaka. The huge Hawaiian let go and the gator surged. Its tail whipped, sending sheets of bloody water high into the air. Its questing jaws locked on to the dead man and tasted blood. With another flick of its giant tail it was off.

Kinimaka sat in the water, strength sapped to the last ounce. Hayden put an arm around his shoulders. Together they ignored the enemy for a few seconds.

Then, Hayden lifted her machine-gun again. The bad guys were about to disembark, leaving them fully exposed. Click. The weapon was empty.

Her head went down. For one second she felt utter despair and rage that she had not been able to live up to her father's dreams. That she hadn't excelled his marvellous legacy.

But no one could say they hadn't given it their all.

Boudreau was gesticulating. The knife he had used to kill her team reappeared in his hands and chopped at the testosterone-charged air.

Then came the sound of hope, of potential reprieve. The thud, thud, thud of heavy machinery. Choppers, fast approaching.

Big, black, and unmistakably military, they came swinging around a bend in the channel like a motorcyclist takes the last bend in a race.

Boudreau screamed, and suddenly his voice was high-pitched with fear. "Move out! Move out! Now, you assholes! Now we'll have to go into hiding!"

Yes, Hayden thought. You failed, you bastard. Try explaining that to the goddamn Blood King.

CHAPTER EIGHT

When Matt Drake first clapped eyes on Hayden Jaye he thought she was already dead. His heart froze in fear, throat tightening as he envisaged what Ben's reaction would be, and then she moved. There was a huge mass beside her and it too was moving. Drake could hardly believe it was a man; its size dwarfed Hayden, but she appeared to be happy sat right next to him.

"The fuck's that?" One of the SEAL team guys said. "A hippo? In the Everglades?"

"That'll be Mano," Ben spoke up for the first time, his eyes and heart alight. "She mentioned he was pretty huge."

"Huge, yeah," came the reply. "Pretty? Nah."

The chopper hovered low whilst men leapt out. Their mission was to reclaim Hayden Jaye, not pursue the enemy, so they showed no interest in the fleeing band of murderers. Ben jumped out too, landing face-first and spluttering and thrashing in the shallow water whilst everyone watched in amusement.

But he wasn't fazed. As soon as he'd planted his feet he used them to forge a path to Hayden's side. Drake was a step behind and heard the words they said to each other.

As did Mano Kinimaka.

Drake and the outsize Hawaiian shared a brief smile and then Hayden was back to business.

"We need to get back to that HQ of theirs. And fast. They cleared out so fast they probably left something behind."

Drake eyed her torn and muddy clothes, the blood that still soaked her hair, the wounds on her face. "Don't take this wrong, Hayden. I know you've just been in a bloody battle. But, are you sure? You look like you're gonna collapse."

"Probably will, Drake. Probably will. But those sadists killed four CIA agents and, believe me, they're after something much bigger. And they work for a guy who's, possibly, the most evil man in history. And that's just his reputation. So, yeah, I'm damn sure."

Slowly, they helped Hayden and Kinimaka towards the thundering chopper. The SEAL team were stationed around the perimeter, keeping watch, but not even the crazy gator showed its head. Within five minutes they were airborne again.

Ben was squeezed as close to Hayden as he could get; his own clothes now wet and dirty. "I feel like I haven't breathed since I last spoke to you," he said in a low voice that everyone pretended they hadn't heard.

Hayden didn't move. "In a different way," she said, "so do I. Look, Ben, I can't do this now. Not yet. They killed my men, murdered them right in . . . in front of me. I won't rest until I've done my best to make sense of their deaths."

The chopper landed back at Boudreau's HQ. Drake let Hayden get off first and let her have her head. He motioned to Ben and Kennedy. "Just let this happen," he told them. "Don't interfere. Even if she collapses on her feet. She needs to exhaust herself."

Kennedy nodded. "Clearly." Ben looked less sure, but agreed when Drake winked. "Best way mate," Drake assured him. "Give her space."

They trooped into the shambolic HQ.

Screams echoed from her cell, hitting her with a peculiar déjà vu.

"What-"

One of the SEAL guys came over to her. "Miss Jaye. We captured one of their operators. He's back there." The man inclined his head. "We're talking to him."

"Let me-"

"It's not Boudreau," Drake stepped up beside her. "Just a geek. A computer guy. Let them work, Hayden."

"They sent him back to destroy evidence and information," the SEAL guy was saying. "So something's here. It would help us, Miss Jaye, if we knew what we were looking for."

Hayden took a moment to catch the man's eyes. "No offence. I can't tell you. It . . . it goes so far up the chain you wouldn't believe."

"Fair enough."

Another rough scream rent the air. Despite herself, Hayden shivered. She turned to Ben. "You're good at this, Blakey. Take a look."

Ben wandered off amongst the destroyed terminals, kicking debris as he went. Drake and Kennedy stayed with her, silent.

"I'll be ok," she said without looking at them. "Not yet. Never the same, probably. But I'll be ok."

Drake nodded, saying nothing. Of them all, the ex-SAS man would know best what she was feeling.

"I've never seen Ben so worried. Never. You mean a lot to him, Hayden."

"I know."

"Might shock you but he's even taken his Taylor poster down off the wall."

Hayden smiled reflexively. "Swift? Or Momsen?"

"Need you ask? In the spirit of Dinorock I'll just quote Motley Crue: Girls, girls, girls. I think one of those is you."

Ben shouted them over. He was kneeling amidst a pile of discarded paper. "I've got some random stuff right here. One of these guys must have been a Johnny Depp fan. Look - a history of Blackbeard the pirate. Grrarrgh! Some bumf about a ship called the Queen Anne's Revenge. Entire reams of shit on the Bermuda Triangle," he said, winking at Drake. "Know what I mean?"

Hayden looked perplexed. "A device was recently salvaged from the wreck of the Queen Anne's Revenge, Blackbeard's ship, which they have in reality been salvaging for what seems like twenty years. It was broadcast on T.V. We think this so-called Blood King saw the broadcast and knew immediately what the device could do, and, more importantly, how it can do what it does." She paused for a moment.

"We don't."

Drake waved a hand around. "And I'm just guessing, but after seeing the amount of firepower around here - and the CIA's reaction to your abduction - that it's a pretty big thing . . . what it does."

Hayden was quiet for one long moment. "The answer to the Bermuda Triangle phenomenon." She said quietly. "But the damn thing's ancient. Truly ancient. It may predate the dinosaurs."

Drake frowned at her. "Eh?"

Kennedy grabbed a sheaf of papers off the floor, now tying her long hair back as she straightened. "Wasn't Blackbeard called the Blood King?"

"I don't know," Hayden looked startled. "Was he?"

"Maybe I got it from a movie," Kennedy said, waving her flippant comment away. "Who knows?"

David Leadbeater

"Well, hopefully the Blood King ain't Blackbeard." Drake tried a chuckle which came out sounding more like a duck arguing with a frog.

"The problem is," Hayden continued, "there may be a second part to the device. A more important piece. And no one knows where that is."

Ben looked up from the litter. "Sounds like a challenge to me."

CHAPTER NINE

The CIA jet skimmed across the purple clouds, flying away from the dark and chasing the light. In a happy mood, Drake likened the allusion to himself and his friend, Ben - two good guys always chasing the light.

They were well on their way to Atlantic Beach, the small U.S. town close to where the decade-long salvage operation had been continuing on the Queen Anne's Revenge, Blackbeard's flagship. Sometime during the flight Ben and Hayden had taken themselves a few rows back for a little privacy, leaving Kennedy and Drake alone.

Drake was feeling a little tense. It wasn't easy even for an ex-soldier to be so close to the action and not get involved. The mood wasn't helped by Justin Harrison, who had placed himself at the front of the plane and was trying to lecture them.

Trouble was, the information he was imparting was imperative. The way he delivered it was somewhat shoddy.

" . . . ship lies in twenty-three feet of water and took over two hundred and fifty years to find. Of course, it wasn't being searched for all that time. Quite the opposite. The North Carolinan . . . "

Drake zoned out. Harrison walked and talked faster than girls used to drop their pants at a Rolling Stones' concert. And still probably do, Drake thought. Jagger still had it. He leaned in to Kennedy and nodded at Harrison. "Sympathy for the devil?"

Kennedy sighed. "He's not a man of taste and means, that's for sure."

They both tried to listen carefully, aware that amidst the blather there might be a gold nugget or two.

" . . . Blackbeard surrendered and accepted a royal pardon for himself and his men. What we don't understand is why, for that brief period, because he soon returned to his pirating ways. It's even more bizarre when you consider he purposely ran aground his flagship – QAR - to surrender in the first place. Act of a madman?" Harrison paused for a millisecond to breathe.

"Blackbeard's various travels are well catalogued, as well as most of his routes. Early assumptions are that he traded the device and its controller along the way. At least once. Maybe many times."

"How so?" Drake shot out the question just to get a break.

"Blackbeard's Claw." Harrison looked please with himself.

"He had a claw?" Mano Kinimaka, situated at the back of the plane, rumbled. "A bit like Captain Hook?"

"Errm, no. Blackbeard's Claw was a man, so called because he was a fierce fighter who led all of Blackbeard's boarding parties. He terrified all men. Blackbeard most likely sold the device for a pretty penny and then sent his second-in-command to take it back."

No one laughed at the pirate half-reference. Drake was regressing and starting to wonder if the jet came equipped with parachutes, when Ben finally spoke up.

"So where did Blackbeard get it?"

Harrison shrugged faster than bolt lightning. "Who knows? Probably robbed it from another pirate. Maybe even from old Hornigold himself - the man who first made Blackbeard captain and gave him a ship called La Concorde, later to be renamed the Queen Anne's Revenge."

"So this device," Ben continued, "you have no idea where it comes from? What exactly does it do?"

"Well, it's a technology far beyond what we possess today," Harrison told them, breathing deeply for a change. "And its origin predates the dinosaurs."

Kinimaka gasped. "Is that possible?"

Drake was growing fond of the lovable jester. "Not unless you believe in aliens," he paused. "Do not tell me this is another bloody alien theory, Harrison."

"No. No. No. There's only one theory-"

At that moment the TV screen behind the secretary's aid switched itself on. "Ah," the man went on, undeterred, "this is the ship as it looks today."

Underwater scenes flashed past - undetermined objects covered in crustaceans, caressed and embraced by the jealous seas for hundreds of years. The scene then switched to what could only be a museum, jam-packed with artefacts.

"Thousands," Harrison said to their surprised faces. "Anything from glass window shards to cannons and the great anchor."

Drake coughed. "So you've figured out the Blackbeard angle. We get that. How about this Blood King? You got anything on him yet?"

Harrison's face revealed the truth before his lips. "We don't know who that is."

Drake gave him a fake look of amazement. "But you're the U.S. government."

"The Blood King is a mythical figure. Doesn't exist."

Kinimaka sounded shocked. "What? Like the dodo?"

"No! Like the damn clitoris!" Ben shouted without thinking, and then sank down in his seat when everyone turned round. Even Hayden forgot her recent trauma for a moment to smirk.

Drake turned the topic back around. "So you're saying this guy's a myth? After all that Hayden's learned for you?"

"We're actively searching for him and, believe me, that's a major understatement. Information on Ed Boudreau, however, is flooding in. We'll get updated when we reach the ship."

The TV screen behind Harrison changed picture and suddenly Secretary of Defence, Jonathan Gates, was sat there, staring at them all.

"Can you hear me on the plane? Hello?"

Harrison died and went to heaven. "Ah, Jonathan. Good to see you. So to speak . . . haha. Well, yes, we hear you, umm . . . loud and clear!"

Gates addressed the team. "Miss Jaye and Mr Kinimaka? Just wanted to say - job well done - under the harshest of conditions. My thoughts are with you, and your lost men, and their families."

"Thank you, sir," Hayden whispered. Kinimaka offered a grunt.

"That being said we now know the kind of enemy we are up against. The notion of an actual Blood King is being looked at very carefully. You guys know the saying - 'the Devil's greatest trick was in convincing the human race that he didn't exist?' Well, I guess we're treating this guy as the devil."

"Wise move," Drake said. "From all I've heard."

"I want your input," Gates said. "I do. Not the United States government, me. There are too many bureaucrats clinging on to this Blackbeard thing right now, and not enough real men. I'll authorise your access and give you what you need to investigate where you see fit. We . . . we all owe you a huge debt of gratitude for the 'Odin thing'."

Drake was fascinated how even a United States senator referred to their previous world-saving quest as the 'Odin thing'. He also concealed a large slice of respect for this man. "We'll start as soon as we land, sir."

The aeroplane started to lose altitude. Drake felt his ears pop.

Jonathan Gates said: "Take a look around the salvage area. Then, we'll transport you to the highly secure area where the device is being overhauled. Let's see what you can do."

Gates smiled. Harrison's return smile would have scared off a T-Rex. Drake sat there, wishing he could answer Wells' most recent call but wary of American ears until he reached the safety of solid ground. A soldier's obstinate principle - and not easily overcome.

And, more importantly - wishing he could answer Mai's latest call. He already missed her delicious, cultured tones caressing his eardrums. And the information she might have, of course.

CHAPTER TEN

After leaving the plane, Drake and the others were transported immediately to a small town called Atlantic Beach. It was offshore of this town, near a preserve called Fort Macon, that Blackbeard's infamous ship lay waiting in shallow water for hundreds of years.

The CIA were pushing this thing hard, Drake thought. By all accounts the so-called 'device' was secured aboard a U.S. Destroyer and guarded by a veritable army of marines. At the airfield they had been cautioned to absolute secrecy and bundled into sleek, black vehicles. Drake didn't mention his recent calls to Wells and Mai, didn't have to. People of that calibre would already know.

Right now, they were passing Fort Macon, a busy state park that surrounds a coastguard base and, despite its seeming remoteness, claimed over a million visitors per year.

"The operation's continuing right over there," Harrison pointed. "We'll take a quick look and then we're heading over to the U.S.S. Port Royal, sent over from its homeport, Pearl Harbor, to take part in the operation."

Kennedy raised an eyebrow at Drake. "By take part, I guess he means commit overkill."

Drake grinned, not only at the comment, but at the way she looked today. Since the death of Thomas

Kaleb, Kennedy had become increasingly more outgoing and accessible. Gone were the body-concealing bland suits. Gone were the torture devices that used to pin her hair back.

Now she sat with her long black hair framing her shoulders, an open smile on her face, and a nice pair of black hipsters that showed off her legs. She sensed Drake staring overlong at her. "What? Seen something ya' like?"

He shrugged his shoulders and made a rocking motion with his hand. "Meh."

They stopped parallel to the big salvage project that was underway around where Intersal Inc. had discovered the Queen Anne's Revenge. It gave Drake a few moments to wonder how to approach the great pair of white elephants: the only things coming between Kennedy and him.

Only things . . . and so far insurmountable.

It had only been six weeks or so, but she hadn't mentioned Kaleb once. Sometimes, at night, he heard her Skype-ing, or on the phone. He fancied she was still in contact with the serial killer's victims' families. Was that a good thing? Would it bring closure?

Or would it bring despair?

His own demons were no less brutal. The memory of Alyson walking out the door, tears in her eyes as she walked to the car. No goodbye. No last wonderful memory. Just those tears, clouding her vision . . . as she drove rapidly towards her fatal accident.

He focused on the present. The salvage crew were aboard a medium-size boat that swayed in choppy seas. There wasn't a whole lot going on, and after a few minutes everyone just looked at Harrison.

The Secretary's aid just shrugged. "It's Blackbeard's ship."

Then he spoke into a wrist-mic. "Let's go."

They sped off, heading for the U.S.S. Port Royal and its world-shaking cargo.

David Leadbeater

CHAPTER ELEVEN

Forty-five minutes later they were being taken board the U.S.S. Port Royal, a Ticonderoga-class cruiser, something Drake knew to be a part of the Navy's ballistic missile defence initiatives. These babies had been commissioned to help intercept and shoot down incoming ICBMs. On the water they were a genuine floating fort, 9000 tons and six hundred feet of sensors and processing systems, armaments and even a few Sikorsky helicopters.

A grey billion-dollar monster, a turbine-propelled death and defence machine.

When they hit the deck Harrison was saying: "This thing's equipped with more sonar and surveillance equipment than anything in the vicinity, even more so than some newer missile cruisers, to be honest. We're lucky it was so close."

Drake stared at the cold steel, the cold eyes of the crew watching them, the hard men with their fingers already on triggers.

My God, he thought. They're acting like we're at war.

Below decks they were shown to separate, Spartan cabins. Harrison left them with a brief: "Thirty minutes," and Drake found himself with some alone time, at last, with his friends.

He went to Hayden first. Not that he had to walk far in the cramped confines since Mano Kinimaka took up half the room.

"There is no doubt we will avenge them. Trust me, Hayden. No doubt."

"Boudreau . . . he's not only a sadist and a murderer, he's damn clever too." Hayden eyes were saturated with pain. "A terrible enemy."

Drake leaned in close. "We'll get him. Trust me."

The words he left unsaid echoed around his brain: I'm a far worse enemy to him than he ever will be to you.

"So what's the verdict?" Ben was saying. "Something still doesn't ring true here," and now he looked at his girlfriend. "They brought all this stuff out of the ocean. Cannons. Anchors. Sounding weights. And nothing happened. Then boom!, they bring up a rusty old box and some mythical monster decides to surface and fight the U.S. military for it who, in turn, decide to guard it with a damned army," Ben spread his arms. "How did everyone know what it was? And, why not go get it before the salvage operation?"

Drake thought about that for a second. "Toddler Blake's got a point."

"Bollocks, crusty."

Hayden shrugged. "For me, it was just another day, another case I pulled. They told me to investigate, so I did. We don't question why."

"And how did Blackbeard, of all people, get involved?" Kinimaka spoke up. "And the alien thing? Bullshit."

"What did you find out?" Drake asked Hayden. "You said it was the answer to the Bermuda Triangle mystery. What is it?"

"I also just found out the damned thing comes in two parts. Two. We have the first. I don't think there's anyone alive who knows where the second part is."

"But what is it?" Kennedy was getting frustrated. "Maybe you could tell us, Mano?" She turned a sweet smile on the giant. Drake shook his head - bemused.

"Boss did go over it," Kinimaka admitted. "Most of it skimmed right over the top of my head, to be honest."

Hayden smiled sweetly. "It's a time displacement device. And it's time we went to see it."

*****

Through the bowels of the great ship they were led. Silent marines with loaded and cocked weapons escorted them front and behind. In Ben's whispered words it almost felt as if they were captives here. The massive cruiser rocked slightly from side to side, its joints and welds groaning like a host of condemned souls.

At last they reached a nondescript door and were ushered inside. True to form, the soldiers lined up outside.

Harrison was already there, pacing faster than some English footballers cheat on their wives. Watching him with wry amusement was one of the ship's officers. A third man was further away, bending slightly to study an object placed on a steel table.

"At last. At last," Harrison beckoned them in, looking sweaty and nervous. "This way. Device is over here."

Drake frowned hard at the aid. "You got somewhere else to be, Justin?"

The aid blinked. "Umm, no. Why?"

Drake waved him on. Kennedy whispered: "Take it easy. Guy's weird, but harmless."

"It's probably me," Drake admitted with a glint in his eye. "I just don't like guys with very small penises."

Hayden blinked in interest, Ben shook his head, and Kennedy bit. "How'd you know . . . ?"

"Break the name down," Drake smirked as he strode ahead. "Just. In."

"Dinosaur," Ben called after him. "That joke's older than York Minster."

Drake approached the metal table. The man next to it straightened and gave him an appraising stare.

Soldier, Drake thought. Commander. Probably in charge of the military forces around here.

"Name's Drake," he said holding his hand out. "Matt Drake."

"As in Bond?" the man let slip a little smile that didn't grace his eyes. "Jo Bradey. SOG."

Drake was rocked, despite himself. The SOG were a small elite force within Delta force. A highly secretive group, not too dissimilar from the command he used to be a part of - the English SRT . He hid his surprise by glancing towards the table.

"So that's the thing that's got everyone's knickers in a twist, eh?"

His friends gathered around him. Before them, given pride of place on an otherwise bare table, sat what at first glance appeared to be a rusty metal box. When Drake bent a little closer, unconsciously imitating the SOG commanders' pose of a minute ago, he was able to distinguish several tiny marks decorating its rough-looking surface.

What at first appeared to be a shabby old hunk of metal was on closer inspection a clever work of art. Indistinct, sweeping whorls covered the entire exterior, each one designed to blend with the next - infinite arches perhaps, or graceful waves of power.

"Fascinating, isn't it?" Harrison was still trying to push things along. "This is the device that was hauled up from the bottom the ocean, from Blackbeard's own cabin, we think. You can see now why it might be traded back and forth during the pirate days."

"And you think this thing has been the cause of random occurrences in the Bermuda Triangle?" Kennedy asked sceptically. "A phenomenon which, as you know, has always been denied and disproven. Until now."

"As it will continue to be," Bradey said. "Half the aeroplanes landing in Orlando travel through the heart of the Triangle. We wouldn't wanna panic folk bound for Mickeyland now would we?"

"They do?" Ben asked. "How many of them know that?"

"Surprisingly few," said Bradey chuckling.

Ben set his jaw. "Look," he said, "there's something you people aren't telling us. How do you know that thing . . . " he waved at the box, " . . . is responsible for causing the Bermuda Triangle? How can you? The phenomenon has never been attributed to anything, ever, so how is it possible now to say - 'oh yeah, this box is the cause.'"

There was a moment's silence that threatened to stretch into something more uncomfortable. Hayden filled the gap eloquently.

"I can explain how the CIA knew that a crappy looking box suddenly went viral and shocked the underworld to its core."

Ben pulled a face. "OK."

"The uplift was filmed on national TV," she said. "Regretfully. The moment that box broke free of the water, the very second it began to spin slowly with all those cameras focused on it, monitored 'chatter' went up five thousand percent."

"Five thousand?" Drake breathed, and even Bradey looked impressed.

"That's how we knew it was something special."

"What type of chatter?" Ben pressed.

"The type that's attributed to bad people in bad regions. The type that's filled with flagged code-words. The type that's passed on through less-than-legal channels. Channels we know about but allow to operate to give us the heads up. Basically, the things the CIA are paid to do."

"Cool." Ben nodded. "I get that now. But . . ."

"Yes, yes, I know - the Bermuda Triangle part. Well . . ." Hayden now seemed a little embarrassed. "There are so many things recorded throughout history. We all know this. What many people don't know is that the CIA employ various people - boffins, super-intellectual geeks, fantasists, professors - just to collect and read all this shit and feed it into a super-computer." She grinned at Ben's expression. "For real. We do. And we're by no means the only U.S. agency or world government that does so."

"It's said they hired a bunch of writers to sketch out various scenarios that the government stiffs would never dream of after 9/11," Kennedy said. "This ain't so far-fetched."

"They did," Hayden said. "We did. The CIA. Anyway, this shit sticks, so to speak, to the grey matter. They found old writings that indicate Blackbeard was in possession of a 'cheap trinket box that fairly made the ground sway and turned a man's legs to jelly'. It went on to describe people just vanishing in the pirate-king's wake, and played a massive part in cementing Blackbeard's fearsome legend and reputation. It also mentioned a second device, a colourful bit of 'swag that might fetch more'n a pretty penny', but no more than that."

Hayden looked scared. "Boudreau knew this second device was a controller. The CIA did not. Now, if that doesn't scare any of you, then I suggest you go home now."

"I get it," Ben said again. "The cheap box is the hard-drive, the engine. The pretty device controls it. So the man who holds both . . ."

". . . Manages a portable displacement device," Drake finished.

"I still don't know how it's responsible for the Triangle phenomenon," Ben stated flatly.

"What we now think is this: that the second device controls the output, the on/off and directionality. But - that the box has juice of its own. And that an unknown chain of events has, quite randomly, set it off several times over the years."

"You do realise what you're telling us?" Drake said to her, already utilizing the old SAS brain for weighing and measuring the ship's defences. "You know what a displacement device is - in plain terms?"

"A time-machine. Yes. And one that can be controlled by the man who acquires both devices."

"The Blood King?" Kinimaka sounded scared, a sentiment that just didn't fit him.

"I can see why a thirty-year-old myth would come out of hiding to acquire such a thing," Bradey said. "For unlimited power. The chance to rule the world through blackmail."

"It predates all known histories," Hayden went on. "Within its makeup are certain elements and minerals that haven't existed since times unknown. So long before the dawn of civilisation it makes the mind boggle."

Drake wondered about that. Hadn't Odin's Shield contained something similar?

Harrison interrupted his thoughts. "It has some of the oldest known constituents ever recorded. We're talking way over 500 million years."

"A lost civilisation?" Kennedy tugged at the waistband of her hipsters, still conscious of her figure, despite herself. "Like Atlantis?"

Hayden suddenly looked tired. "Who knows? And, frankly, who cares? Where it came from is not the issue here."

"Well said," said Drake nodding. He then looked the SOG commander dead in the eyes. "How good are you and your men, Bradey?"

"We have two full units here, Drake. Plus two hundred marines, Delta Force and other select companies. God couldn't get into this room."

"It's not God I'm worried about. It's a man who's managed to convince the entire world for about thirty years that he's just a myth," he said, grimacing at Hayden. "And I'm sorry to say, that includes your super-geeks and your 'chatter-monitors' and all the rest of it."

"A goddamn Transformer couldn't get in here." Bradey was starting to sound annoyed, but smoothed it over with a little grin. "Though I daresay Megan Fox might sneak through."

There were a few moments while all the men considered the scenario before conversation caught up again.

"Time travel," said Kennedy, who was again tugging up her jeans whilst contemplating the box on the table. "Has anyone given this thing a shake?"

Harrison gawped. "Are you kidding?"

Kinimaka looked sick. "Didn't you see Terra Nova?"

Drake's mind was still trying to get into sync with his enemies'. "Ok, so the logical next step is to search for the second device. To hold either piece will negate the effect of the other device. To hold both-"

he left that hanging, aware that the U.S. government was strongly represented in the room.

"That's the dilemma. No one knows where to start." Hayden's smile was tired and drawn. Nightmares of the last few days still moved in her eyes.

Drake said, "You start with the last place they were seen together. And then you follow whatever trail you can."

"Been there," Ben smiled. "Done that."

Hayden gave him a forlorn look. "Is that another Dinorock tune. Don't tell me they've got you doing it too."

"No!" Ben's shout was loud enough to make the marines stationed by the door glance around. "I will never join the Dinorock crew, Hey! You know that."

"Look," said Bradey as he started to walk away, his motion designed to break up their little party, "you're not the only people working on this. Gut feeling? Someone's gonna get lucky. I hope it's you guys."

Harrison took the unspoken hint. Quickly he lifted his huge briefcase and, despite its awkward bulk, took off at a fast pace.

Drake blinked at Ben. "I know what I said, mate, but I'm just the muscle here. Where the hell do we start?"

Ben opened his mouth to speak, but before he could express himself there was an explosion so loud they all looked up to see if the roof was caving in on them.

The entire ship shuddered.

Bradey was already on his wrist mic. He looked dumbfounded. "This ship is under attack," he said in utter disbelief. "Under attack."

CHAPTER TWELVE

For a long moment Drake and his friends stared at each other. Bradey took his marines and raced off, the shock of it all still apparent in his voice as he barked out orders.

Drake regarded the box. "Last place we wanna be."

He moved into the passageway. The fading footsteps of the racing marines still echoed from the bland walls.

"Remember the way out?" Kennedy asked.

Drake shot her a 'don't be silly' look and set off. Moving blindly like this and with limited cover and escape routes, he felt extremely uncomfortable. Bradey needed his bollocks tweaking for not leaving them a gun. Harrison was blethering on, only further confusing the ex-SAS man's radar.

"Let's keep it down," he rasped along the line. "We have no idea what we're dealing with here."

"I do." Hayden said softly. "Boudreau."

Drake paused and looked along the line. At the back stood the man-mountain, Kinimaka. His steely eyes met Drakes' and expressed just one word.

Revenge.

Drake moved off. "I'll tell you this, Hayden. Boudreau ain't the hardest man on this vessel."

The passageway ran straight for twenty feet before hitting a ninety degree junction. Signage was noticeably absent. Drake felt a moment of frustration and then turned right, almost sure it led to their cabins from which he could easily find the deck.

The odd thing was they walked in utter silence. On board a ship of hundreds he heard not a single voice. Creepy thoughts of the Bermuda Triangle entered his head.

At last they reached their cabins. As Drake paused to have a quick look a second intense explosion shook the U.S. cruiser, making the walls and the floor shiver and shake.

"Above decks could be worse," Kennedy said.

"Now, maybe," Drake told her. "But if those guys made it down here we'd be gravy."

"Down here?" Hayden looked shocked. "How could they ever get down here? There's a boatful of U.S. marines to get through."

"But they already knew that," Drake said. "And yet still . . . they're attacking this ship."

The ex-soldier led them on, trying to exercise speed and caution and, at last, they were standing before a set of stairs that led up to the deck. Now, the sounds of combat were more apparent.

"Seriously," Kennedy reiterated, "wouldn't it be easier to hold them off down here."

Drake felt a moment's frustration. He was trying to save their lives. Questions weren't helping. "Stop thinking a step ahead," he said shortly, "and try thinking four or five steps ahead. They will have planned for that contingency. Now follow!"

Boots hammering the steps, he pounded upwards, cracked open the door and glanced out. One . . . two . . . three. Five seconds, then he ducked back in.

"Ship's clean," he said. "No bad guys. The marines are holding them off."

He cracked the door again and they filed out. The big five-inch gun mounted on the bow was before them. Behind them bristled the various radar arrays towers and illuminators. The deck was jammed with hard-faced marines. Alarms and sensors were going off everywhere.

But Drake read the confusion behind their eyes and saw the panic they were concealing at the shrieking warning bells and stopped dead. "Don't like the look of this."

He started towards the big gun and then something happened that made the British seen-it-all SAS soldier stand and gawp like a three-year-old on a visit to Disneyland.

Above the bow, above the massive gun, above the port and starboard side, and rising like prehistoric moths appeared at least a dozen choppers. In less than a second they all opened fire. The sound of metallic hell filled the air so loudly that Drake found himself unable to think.

He fell to the deck and crawled. As his senses returned he glanced underneath his own body. His friends were in a similar state, stunned into immobility. Bullets clanged and whined and ricocheted off every metal surface - a category-five hurricane of lead that tore through skin and bone and left men screaming in its wake.

Drake looked up when it stopped, relieved to be in one piece. Half a dozen helicopters were drifting over the ship, rappel lines unravelling. Drake foretold the future and scrambled quickly for a discarded weapon. There were plenty about. The carnage around him was indescribable. At least three-quarters of the downed men were still alive, in various states of hurt, but there was nothing he could do for them now.

It was kill or be killed, and this was his stage.

"Stay with me!" He ran instinctively for the side of the boat where he knew life-rafts were positioned. Emergency escape. That was all they had in their favour now.

But quicker than he would have believed possible the rappel lines quivered and men were landing lightly on deck all around them. Drake punched the first hard in the face, the second he clubbed with the machine-gun.

Many marines were still functioning and began to fight. A melee erupted on deck, gun-battle and hand-to-hand fighting of the most violent kind.

Drake led his small party through the middle of it. Mano Kinimaka bulldozed straight into a gathering group of enemy combatants, scattering them like bowling balls.

"Run, damn you!"

The life-rafts were about ten feet away. All of a sudden Drake saw half a dozen bouncing grenades litter the deck.

It was then that the war really began.

CHAPTER THIRTEEN

"Dive!" Drake screamed, hoping everyone got the message. He felt Ben hit the deck by his side, groaned as Kennedy landed on his legs, and thanked his lucky starts it hadn't been Kinimaka. Explosions ripped through the ship. Soldiers died on both sides, twisting and yelling as they collapsed.

Drake grunted again as one of the enemy landed on him, having bore the brunt of the shrapnel that was heading his way. Still, a few shards tore through Drake's skin, causing a searing pain that he ignored.

He pushed to his knees. They had to get to the life-rafts. Their survival depended on it. But around the corner of the steel radar column they hit serious obstructions. Marines were taking cover among the girders, both at deck-level and further up amongst the tree-like stanchions. Bullets pinged from surface to surface faster than a man's eyes move at a women's beach volleyball tournament.

Bradey was in the midst of it, firing and shouting orders through his radios, trying to hold together a makeshift team of some of the best men in the world who, in a matter of minutes, had been sent reeling.

That was the key factor here, Drake thought. Not skill or bravery, but shock and awe - the Americans being played at their own game on their own soil. By Christ, there would be some repercussions.

The life-rafts were effectively cut off. And the battle behind them was only getting fiercer and closer. Drake knew the only way to protect his people was to fully engage in this fight. He fired his weapon at the men slithering down the ropes. Enemy bodies fell and crashed to the deck. The sound of breaking bones made even the hardest man wince. Some bad guys paused in mid-fall to level their weapons and fire a few bursts in Drake's direction, but their aim was spoiled by the sway of the ropes.

Kennedy snatched up a gun and started firing.

Ben ducked behind them as a metal sleet drove above their heads. Luckily, the raucous sound of his mobile ringing distracted the enemy more than Drake and his friends.

"Sis?" He answered it without thinking. "Karin? Yeah, yeah, not bad. Look-"

Drake dived left, hitting the deck in a roll and came up firing. More bodies somersaulted from the skies, trailing fountains of blood, and came crashing down amongst their own brethren below.

"No," Ben was saying, "I'm in the States. Look . . . what? What's wrong with seeing Hayden?"

A man had surprised Kennedy, sneaking up behind her amidst the turmoil and strong-arming her around the neck. She struggled, bucking and kicking fiercely, suddenly reminded of her contest with Thomas Kaleb in the battle arena, reminded of that rank smell, those evil, blood-smeared hands. How he touched her. How he drooled on her . . .

Fight!

The inner voice, so loud and commanding, was pure self-preservation. She lifted her body, using her attacker as a fulcrum, and then swung all her weight backwards, still holding the light machine-gun.

Her heels crashed into his shins, making him buckle but not relent. The butt of her gun jabbed his ribs. The back of her head, on the return swing, then smashed against his forehead with stunning force.

The man staggered away. Kennedy turned and mercilessly opened fire, sending his body reeling against the bulkhead.

Ben was on his knees, eyes a centimetre away from deck, looking for all the world as if he had found a new breed of insect on a still, sunny day in the calmest meadow. "Karin. I hear you, but Hayden's alright. She's good for me-"

The soldier Kennedy had shot landed face down beside him, broken and bloody. The knife he had been holding but never gotten the chance to use bounced off Ben's head and struck the floor.

"She's CIA," Ben said with a dollop of sarcasm. "Not Marine Force Recon!"

Drake allowed himself to join the fray again instead of keeping half an eye on Kennedy's struggle. The deck was crowded now, much of it covered in pitch battle. One thing was obvious to Drake - the cavalry, by now, would be well on its way.

So that pointed to another, more-important thing - the attackers and Boudreau, if the sadistic murderer was indeed behind this - would have planned for all this. Thus they would more than likely already have secured the device.

All we have to do is hang on, he thought. We can't escape, we just have to live.

"That way." He pointed back past the door they had come through. There was a corner bulkhead and a storage bin over there - meagre coverage but better than their current position.

They scooted across. Drake made to grab an opponent who was in their way, but Mano Kinimaka beat him to it, bulldozing past and ramming a stiff arm into the guy's head. It was instant lights-out for their adversary, and a better way out for him than Drake had been planning.

As he ran, Drake sought to help his fellow soldiers by firing single shots at their rivals, relieving pressure, saving lives, backing the team. His own mobile had vibrated twice, and that meant either Wells or Mai, or both.

Another explosion, and this time fire and frag blasted past the corner they had just vacated. A member of Bradey's SOG squad tumbled into view and lay without moving.

"Watch that corner," Drake instructed as he now moved carefully to the starboard side of the ship and peered over the railings. If he had been expecting aircraft carriers, a deadly armada or swarms of choppers he was hugely disappointed. Beyond the choppy, wide seas and the foggy shore in the distance there was nothing to see. He had to assume Boudreau's assault and getaway crew lay to the port side.

How on earth were they ever going to escape?

Hayden was breathing shallowly beside him. She nudged his shoulder. "It's the same set-up as back at the safe house, Matt. Overwhelming surprise. I tell you, there's more than one insider helping them here."

"Stunning," said Drake shaking his head. "I've never heard of anything like this. Look, Hayden, we're soldiers, but they're not." He nodded at Ben and Kennedy. "We need to help the marines from here and just survive. Boudreau's men have to depart soon."

"With the box!" Hayden looked like she was about to head below decks.

"Lost," Drake said. "For now."

Ben's voice was starting to rise. "Karin! I'll call you back. You just can't talk to me like that!"

Hayden's eyes held a depth of pity that suddenly made Drake scared for Ben. "He's a great kid," the ex-soldier said quickly. "His family mean the world to him."

"As my father meant to me," Hayden returned. "But he's gone, and all I have are some memories of him. Funny, how such loving feelings can fade with time, leaving you knowing you had them, but not remembering the overwhelming depth of them."

"Your father," Drake said. "He was CIA wasn't he?"

"James Jaye. J.J.," Hayden said with pride. "If I do nothing else with my life I will honour his death."

Ben was well and truly in second place with this one, Drake thought. How naive of him to think of them as the happy couple, living among the roses and not sensing the coming blight.

Kinimaka now hunched down beside them. "So," he said. "What are we looking at?"

"Water, water everywhere and not a boat to sink," Drake said before rising to his feet. Kinimaka just stared. Drake took a moment to shoot two adversaries who dared to peer around the bulkhead and then checked his weapon.

Three-quarter empty. "Where the hell are the marines?" he wondered aloud.

Then Hayden screamed, making Drake almost squeeze the trigger in alarm. A chopper had been drifting towards them, inch by inch, and now as it came within their warning range a man had leaned out and started shooting.

"Boudreau?" Drake guessed.

"The very motherfucker," Kinimaka growled. "Fruit-bat crazy, that one. Pure fruit-bat."

A great claxon went off, louder than the shooting and the fighting and the death-cries of wounded men. It could only mean one thing. They had the device. Then ropes unravelled heavily from the chopper and struck the deck like big boa-constrictors all around them. All of a sudden men were abseiling down.

Were they trying for Hayden again?

Drake fired the machine-gun one handed, scooping up a knife with the other and walking towards the landing zone. Dead adversaries plummeted to the ship's deck, bouncing hard.

Hayden emptied her clip too quickly, panic affecting her aim. This arsehole Boudreau really had her traumatized, no doubt his intentions when he so brutally executed her men.

Kinimaka walked with them, waiting for the hand-to-hand. He didn't have to wait long. Their enemies bounced lightly and sprang forward. Drake allowed one to land on his knife, then twisted and slashed another across the throat. He caught a blow on his chest and fired close-up, sending a man skidding back into his comrades, scattering and confusing them.

A knife flashed.

Drake let it pass through the gap between his arm and his chest without even blinking. The knife-wielder's expression change from smug to terrified in a millisecond. It changed to agony one millisecond later.

Kinimaka was at his side, an intimidating presence if ever there was one. Boudreau was leaning out of the chopper, being held up there only by his men, spittle flying from his lips.

"Get him!" came the mad scream. "Can't you fucksticks see him? He's fuckin' big enough!"

Mano? Drake thought. They were after Mano Kinimaka? Not Hayden?

"He's desperate," Kennedy's voice came from close by. "The Blood King must have given him another chance."

More men came at them. Drake understood better now why they weren't shooting. They wanted the

Hawaiian alive. Never mind, it would accelerate their downfall.

He front-kicked one man in the chest, heard ribs break. To his left and right, Kinimaka and Hayden used close-up fighting techniques. Boudreau's team was good, and the melee soon turned into a stalemate, helped at Drake's end by the limited corridor of attack his enemies were afforded by the bulkhead.

Again the claxon sounded. "Fuck you!" Boudreau's voice rang out, a madman on the verge of losing his last, tentative grip on reality. "Fucking useless meatheads!"

And he started shooting indiscriminately. Several of his men went down. Blood slathered the deck. Boudreau laughed. "Fucking," he fired, killing a young mercenary with red hair. "Useless," he fired again, sending another bullet into another subordinate. "Meatheads!" He fired twice more. Two more men collapsed, one with a hole in his head and his blood spattered across the rest of the living.

"Get back! Are you deaf as well as useless?"

The remaining men started to jog towards the port side. They must have some kind of makeshift disembarkation apparatus over there.

Which is why they were defending that area so ruthlessly against Bradey and his men.

Drake let them go. He had no interest in chasing down fleeing men. The chopper above them with its crazy occupant veered upwards and began to climb.

Hayden was staring at Kinimaka. "What gives, Mano. Why'd that monster want you?"

CHAPTER FOURTEEN

The stakes had risen higher than ever and still they had no idea which mastermind was orchestrating the humiliation of the United States on its own soil.

The SOG commander, Bradey, was alive and looking flabbergasted. He seemed to have lost control of his reasoning abilities. All he could say repeatedly was that someone had declared war against the U.S. military inside its own damn country.

Who would have the resources? Drake wondered. Who would possess such audaciousness? There were people out there who could do it, and he betted that almost every one of them was currently trying to contact the CIA to assure them it wasn't me.

"All of DC will be involved in this now." Hayden had said something, Drake fancied, just to shut Bradey and his rambling up. "And the device that was stolen? That's huge."

"I'll say," Ben agreed with her. "I just got off the phone with dad. He says it's already hit Sky News. Jeremy Thompson looks gobsmacked."

"Poor old Jeremy," Drake said. "One thing's for sure though, if the Blood King now has the box, then he's not going to waste any time before chasing after the controller."

"Everyone will," Kinimaka said.

Ben's mobile sang out a Pretty Reckless song. He moved away to answer it. "Karin?"

Drake ignored Hayden's long look and muttered something about taking a leak. Kennedy was involved with a fallen marine. The man looked so young, lying there trying to look so tough, and all the while back in Montana or Alabama, or plain old Texas, his family were unaware that their son and brother and friend was sharing his final moments with a stranger.

Drake disappeared below to check his mobile. He was right. Wells had tried him twice, Mai just the once. He hit 'return' and waited.

"How ya doin' pal? I'm betting you're near that ship, am I right? The Drakester I knew never strayed far from a battle."

"Not by choice, Wellsy old chap," Drake laid on the jabber. "What do you have for me?"

"Ed Boudreau is a mercenary, plain and simple. The gentleman has all the usual accolades. Even more so now, since he just rammed it up the Yanks' arses. I have a full dossier on the man, but squat-a-doodle-do on the person he works for."

"Nothing?" Drake could hardly believe it. "MI5. SAS. Her Majesty's Secret Service. A dozen secret agencies and you have zilch?"

By now the cold dread Drake had been experiencing, an emotion quite alien to him, was turning into something icier. "Who in God's name is this Blood King?"

"It's an ongoing op, old pal." Wells had waved the question and its sentiment away, clearly either not understanding or not wanting to hear the undertone in it. "Now look, . . . me and my Mai time refuse to be kept waiting much longer. How'd you like some company?"

"You?" Drake coughed. "Why?"

"Umm, expertise. Moral support. General fatherly brilliance. You know."

Drake was going to offer the standard Brit reply up yours, but their situation and what he already knew about the two devices gave him pause. "Do it," he said after a moment. "Contact me when you get to Miami. I'll let you know where we are."

"Excellent." The connection went dead.

Drake stared hard at the mobile, throat suddenly dry. He scrolled down and again clicked 'return'.

"I take it you are alive then, soldier boy." The voice was like a feather's touch on soft skin.

"It'll take much more than a rag-tag army to kill me."

"Your . . . friends?"

He knew she meant well, but also knew the focus of her question revolved around Kennedy. "All good," he said. "Any news?"

"The Bermuda Triangle op . . . " she launched straight into her spiel, ". . . was carried out by the CIA after an unidentified box was uplifted from the ocean depths. You know all the pirate details, I am sure. This op was sanctioned by the Director and classed as a Special Operation. Six of their best agents were teamed together."

She didn't have to say four of whom are now dead.

"The box was examined and classified as a 'time displacement device'. Origin unknown. It was thought it could cause critical anomalies at random intervals, most likely when triggered by a chain of events."

"I know all this, Mai-" Drake said gently.

"The second device," Mai went on, "and don't interrupt me, Matt. Only the rude and the ignorant and

89

the uneducated interrupt. The second device is a controller. It is believed it could actually dictate a time when the box could be turned on. The second device looks like a clock. An ornate clock."

Now Drake took notice. "An expensive-looking clock? It makes sense. Blackbeard might have traded it for a fortune, intending to reacquire it later. Thank you, Mai. Anything else?"

"Nothing that is clear, Drake. I am currently inside the States myself. I will still be able to use my contacts though."

"One other thing," Drake said. "One of the surviving agents is a man by the name of Mano Kinimaka. Maybe you could help us understand why the Blood King wants him captured alive."

"Ah, the Blood King," Mai breathed as if savouring the name and the myth. "He is next on my list. I will let you know the results of my search, my friend."

"Ok," he hesitated. "Mai? I know I don't need to tell you this, I really do. But, please be careful. The Blood King seems to have more resources than God. Don't put yourself in harm's way again. For me."

"Again?" Mai laughed, the sound high and sweet.

"Again. Never again." Drake broke the connection and placed his head against the cold metal wall. Times were hard enough without resurrecting what had gone before with Mai.

Things that should never be spoken about again.

CHAPTER FIFTEEN

After the metaphoric dust had settled, Drake and his friends sought out Justin Harrison and told him what they were planning.

"We're going down to Miami," Drake said. "This whole thing's Caribbean-related. We can work from there and see where the research takes us."

Harrison looked preoccupied. "Yes, yes. Do whatever you must. Just, please-" he met Drake's eyes. "Do it fast."

Dry land beckoned and forty minutes later they were ensconced in a big station-wagon courtesy of the U.S. government, taking a last look through darkened windows at the U.S.S. Port Royal and its shattered hull. The authorities still didn't know how Boudreau and his army had pulled it off, but meticulous planning, advance knowledge, and major inside help were being blamed.

"Jesus," Hayden said as she ended yet another call. "It wouldn't surprise me if there were public executions when this thing comes out!"

"We all love a conspiracy," Kennedy said. The New Yorker was sitting beside Drake in the front, squirming around as she tried to tug the waist of her jeans a bit higher.

"They ain't gonna fall off," Drake frowned at her. "At least, not until we find a hotel."

"Damn things are cut so low I keep showing my damn ass off."

"Well, if we find ourselves chasing the enemy on bicycles your ass crack will make a nice bike park, love."

Kennedy swatted him and finally managed to tug the material where she wanted it.

"Now that's done," Drake sniffed, "maybe we can get back to that what we do best, eh?"

"Saving the world?" Ben read his mind.

"You got it."

The station-wagon cut through the encroaching night with Drake following the SatNav directions to Wilmington International airport. The early November cold snap, so apparent back in the U.K., hadn't made it to this part of the States yet - if it ever did - so Drake drove with the Air Con cranked high. They made one stop to load up on service-station food, Mountain Dew and hot coffee before hitting the road in earnest.

"So," Drake said after a while, "Mano. What did Boudreau want with you, my friend?"

Kinimaka shifted uncomfortably and Drake actually had to make a correction to the car's course. "Beats me," he rumbled. "Far as I know I'm a pretty normal guy."

Hayden had squashed herself in beside him, with Ben to her right. "Trusting, supportive, effective. Is that normal for a guy, Kennedy?"

The only answer was a chortle.

"People you've hurt. Arrested. Places you've been. Men you've crossed. Any stand out at all?"

"Usually, I'm the second, or third in a team. None of the bad guys even know I'm there," he paused. "Unless I hit 'em, I guess. Never had a threatening letter. Lived all my life in Hawaii, north shore Oahu."

"His name in Hawaiian," Hayden said with glint in her eye. "Means 'passionate lover'."

Now Kennedy did turn around. "You're kidding?"

Kinimaka shuffled again, looking embarrassed. "Or 'shark'."

"Or what? I mean, can't they decide?"

Kinimaka shrugged. "Never knew."

"I think we're getting off track," Drake said more gruffly than he wanted to. "You say you're a nobody, a back-up man from hang-loose Hawaii. What the hell would Boudreau want with you?"

"Or more than likely his boss," Kennedy put in. "Boudreau's just a mercenary."

"True."

"So," Ben interrupted, "this convo's getting us nowhere. Are we gonna find this bad-boy controller down in Miami or what?"

"That's the idea," Drake grumbled. "Who rattled your cage, anyway?"

"No one. It'll be fun."

"Nothing about this is fun," Hayden snapped. "People have died."

Ben stared at the floor. "Yeah. Umm, sorry. I didn't mean anything."

David Leadbeater

The uncomfortable silence stretched until Drake broke it. "Either way, we need this controller. We know the bad guys are after it, and that they're after Mano. Let's keep it frosty out there."

In the darkness next to him he felt Kennedy smile, then giggle. Ben whispered 'frosty?' with exaggerated surprise. Even Hayden let out a little chuckle.

Drake gave them a grumpy look. "Just stay alert."

CHAPTER SIXTEEN

For the second time in three days they landed at Miami International, sleep-deprived, shaken and starting to smell a little. The first thing they did was book back into the Fontainbleu, on the Agency's dollar.

"Six hours," Drake told them. "Meet at our room. We'll formulate a plan."

Kennedy and he, alone for the first time in days, entered their room and took a quick look around. All was well. Drake locked the door and set up a booby trap in the form of folded towels to hinder door movements and glasses to give warning whilst Kennedy drew the curtains.

"Normally I like to make love with the curtains open," Drake said in mock complaint. "Whenever I'm in Miami."

"Yeah?" Kennedy came over and threw herself on the deep, plush mattress, fully clothed. "Believe me, you ain't gettin' any until I've had some sleep, soldier-boy."

She turned her back on him. Drake breathed a sigh of relief. The only thing he wanted to do now was to sink into oblivion.

Lights out.

*****

When does six hours feel like six minutes? Drake thought. When you've flown from the U.K. to Miami, landed yourself in the middle of a fire-fight and then flown back to Miami. That's when.

They were barely awake when the first knocks sounded at the hotel room door. Drake yelled a warning, coming awake fast, like he used to in a previous life.

Poised like a cat, eyes searching for prey.

Kennedy grunted and turned over. "Christ, man. What the hell ya doin'?"

He jumped out of bed without answering. The tatters of a hard dream still spun through his subconscious. Nothing he wanted to talk about.

Or remember.

A few minutes later and the hotel room was crowded. Coffee was percolating loudly and happily, but no one held out too much hope for the hotel brand.

Ben sat at the well-polished desk and opened his laptop. "We should start with Google," he said. "And work our way around."

Drake leaned against the wall, switching his attentions between Ben and Collins Avenue, thirty floors down. How many were going about their daily business below him, knowing nothing of the time-displacement device? How many had ever heard of Ed Boudreau and the Blood King?

"So Blackbeard was pretty much a sailor until sometime around 1716," Ben finally spoke up after a lot of tapping and clicking. "Then he met a man called Benjamin Hornigold. After a short time the two began to commit serious acts of piracy. Later, their fleet was boosted by the arrival of another pirate, called-" more tapping. "Umm, Bonnet. Some kind of gentleman pirate. This guy owned extensive lands but chose to become a pirate. Crazy loon."

"Once a scallywag," Drake intoned.

"Shut it, crusty. It goes on . . ." Ben rattled the keyboard happily.

During all this, Drake noticed, Hayden had fielded two calls. Judging by her words and reactions he guessed neither one was good. So, whilst Ben continued his search, Drake wandered over to her part of the room.

"They find out where all those soldiers disappeared to yet?"

"Boudreau's men? They sure didn't vanish into the dang Triangle. He left them. We've picked up many stragglers. To a man they swear Boudreau's their boss. No knowledge of any Blood King."

"It's what I'd say. It's also how I'd operate if I were the Blood King and wanted to stay a myth. Who got away?"

"Boudreau took the device and a few hand-picked men. They left the rest floating to face the music."

Drake whistled. "Man's a total whack-job. Obviously he doesn't care about making enemies."

"I doubt he sees much beyond his own psychotic ego," Hayden looked away for a moment.

"Anything else?"

David Leadbeater

"My boss," the CIA lady admitted. "Wants me on trauma counselling or sick leave or something. He agreed to let me continue when I told him I was engaged in research and, after all, we are in the middle of a crisis."

Hayden pinched the bridge of her nose. Trauma counselling or not, the deaths of her colleagues would haunt her until her dying day.

Ben started up again. Drake turned to listen. Several things quickly became apparent. All three men had worked the pirate trade routes consistently between 1716 and 1718. They had murdered, plundered and bartered thousands if not hundreds of thousands of articles between them, and no doubt with many others like them. Then Hornigold retired, Bonnet was killed, and later so was Blackbeard himself.

Ben spent some time delving into the odd anomaly of Blackbeard's apparent salvation - the time he accepted a royal pardon only to return to piracy soon after.

"That one's hidden deep," Ben said. "Or not here at all." He switched his attentions around, now bombarding the internet with queries and flashing off one Web site and on to another faster than Drake could even read. Some of the cleverer links were embedded near the bottom of the pages, a trick Ben already knew, but something that might have fooled someone just a bit older.

Blackbeard, or Edward Teach, came by the ship he re-named Queen Anne's Revenge when he

98

broadsided a French merchant vessel. Later, he equipped her with 40 guns, turning her into a vessel fearsome enough to match its leader.

An image of Blackbeard flashed up on screen. The blurb described him as immensely tall and wide, and said he was known to place live fuses or matches underneath his hat and then light them when he went into battle, creating a most ferocious spectacle indeed. Edward Teach clearly understood the value of an intimidating appearance.

Kinimaka was reading over Ben's shoulder. "Throw into the mix his right-hand man, the claw, and you have the makings of a legend that lives strong to this very day."

Digging deeper now, Ben pursued every trail that promised even a glimpse into Blackbeard's rich history. It turned out he had many friends, wealthy friends, who owned lands and held influence everywhere. He was well travelled. Jamaica, Grand Cayman, Havana, Florida, South Carolina.

"Is there no direct information?" Kennedy was asking. "About what he traded? Where?"

"Pirates didn't keep records," Ben said. "The best we can hope for is some reference made in a journal or something. Just a matter of trawling through."

Drake got coffee. It was about now in this kind of operation when he started to want to hit bad guys. His military life had taught him to achieve his objective through hard and direct action. Standing around a hotel room - nice as it was, drinking coffee with his friends - pleasant as they were, did nothing to alleviate a rising dread of the consequences of inactivity.

"Blackbeard certainly had his contacts," Ben was saying. "Say's here he spent nights with some of the most notorious boys of the time - Israel Hands, Charles Vane and even Calico Jack. Even I've heard of him."

"Nothing else?" Drake's impatience got the better of him.

"Go take a nap, crusty. Stop hovering or get slapped."

Drake smiled. "Hit me with your best shot, Blakey."

"Oh, good one," Kennedy almost clapped. "Pat Benatar. Loved her."

"Actually, this is interesting. Calico Jack was a snake even among pirates. He deposed Charles Vane and made off with his ship. Sailed with two women, including the notorious Anne Bonny. Jeez, even married her. He is responsible for the famous Jolly Roger skull and crossed swords design."

"Great. Did he carry a time machine?"

"No. But he did employ a man who took down records of his exploits. A vain pirate, that Calico Jack. Now here, I think, is the passage that Hayden's geek-squad found: ' . . . that Edward Teach brought forth two boxes, one of shiny and magnificent lustre and one of cheap design. But when joined, imagination would struggle to conjure a more Hell-like image. The very ground did begin to swell and shake and with mine own eyes I did see some folk vanish as if they had never existed . . . ' That's the pay-dirt the CIA found."

"Good," Drake nodded. "So what does that tell us?"

"Well, it's dated early 1716. That's near the beginning of Blackbeard's career, my friend, so we start from this point in time. This is before he traded the controller and confirms that he had both devices at the same time and that he connected them, somehow. Was he told how? Did he guess? We'll never know."

Ben was still scrolling, still delving, clicking link after link and returning to his original page to start again.

"Well, this is certainly interesting."

Hayden looked up. "What?"

"Something your boffins didn't notice. Look here . . ."

The eighteen-year-old hit a link hidden beneath a highlighted letter towards the end of the passage. The laptop flashed upon a new page. And the headline practically roared at them.

'Read John Bostock's full account of the meeting of Blackbeard and Calico Jack! Visit the Pirates Museum of Nassau, off Bay Street. Closed Public Holidays.'

"Full account?" Hayden repeated. "Are you saying that this isn't a full account, then? I wasn't told about that."

"Because they don't know. They didn't dig far enough."

Drake stared at the screen. "I'm lost. How do you know it's not the full account?"

"Positively? I don't. But look at it. Jeez, it's just a few lines long. You think the meeting of two of the most infamous men who ever lived is worth a crappy half-dozen lines? I don't."

"Munchkin's got a point." Drake conceded, almost unaware he'd spoken aloud.

Mano Kinimaka pricked his ears up. "Nassau? They have a Hard Rock Cafe there don't they?"

Hayden stared at him, clearly trying to make sense of it. "What?"

"I collect shot glasses. We go . . . I get a two-for . . ."

Drake shot him down. "You been pondering my question?"

Kinimkaka looked hurt. Hayden frowned at the Englishman. "Back off, Drake. Mano's the real thing. I vouch for him." Her eyes met Drake's, resolute.

"Fair enough." Drake switched the subject instantly. "Look, it's one in the afternoon. My suggestion - let's see if we can get on the last ship to Nassau, sleep on board, and be fresh by morning."

"Might be slim pickings at this time," Kennedy guessed. "And expensive."

Drake shrugged. "We'll take what we can get."

CHAPTER SEVENTEEN

The ship they boarded, at the last minute, could have been renamed RustBucket without even hurting the owner's feelings. But the food was free, along with the alcohol until 7 p.m., so they decided to take the night off.

Drake and Kennedy took their fancy-free cocktails to one of the ships feeble-looking railings and watched the ocean for a while. Drake tried several different ways of drinking but, in the end, conceded that the only way to actually get a real swig was to throw the multi-coloured umbrellas and cocktail sticks overboard.

Kennedy looked a little lost. "What the hell am I doing?"

"Living on the edge!" Drake squawked, Steve Tyler style.

"Don't. Even your mouth's not that big. I mean, where's my career gone? I haven't seen New York in months, let alone my boss."

"You've started a new career."

"I guess."

"Don't sound too enthusiastic."

"I never do."

"Oh, I dunno," Drake said slyly. "I've heard a few enthusiastic shouts from you."

"I don't need to be here," Kennedy turned to him. "I - we - could be anywhere."

"Could we? Knowing what you know, Kennedy. Could you just leave all this for the CIA to take care of?"

"They're good at what they do. I should be moving forward."

"Not what I meant. The problem is the Blood King. And not who he paid off, but how many he paid off. Imagine a man who would hire Boudreau as a side-kick with enough power to hold the world to ransom."

Kennedy tugged at her jeans and then gave him a quick smile. "Wanna get some enthusiasm going?"

"Mmm. Let's try to do something about those jeans of yours."

*****

Hayden didn't want to think. She said her goodnights to Kinimaka and then took a bottle of Jim Bean and a fistful of Ben's T-shirt and dragged him back to their room. The JB was a third empty by the time she got his pants down; another huge swig and she'd driven him to the corner of the room. Fully clothed, she undressed him and watched the expression in his eyes turn from shock, to pleasure, to lust.

The alcohol burned away the stink of memory, like a blunt knife scraping away congealed blood. Ben's body responded to her touch. To his credit he seemed to realise she was using him and he accepted it. Who wouldn't, she thought with gruff humour.

She climbed on top of him, blonde hair scraping his thighs and belly and then framing his face. "Make me forget them," she said in a small, out-of-character voice. "I need them out of my head. If only for a little while."

Ben stepped up.

*****

Nassau was already in view before Drake surfaced from below decks. He made a point of tugging Kennedy's jeans up for her before she climbed the short ladder in front of him. She smiled back. "Cheeky bastard."

He blinked. "Hey, you're sounding more and more like a proper Yorkshire lass every day."

"New York bitch 'til I die," she whipped back. "And then some."

The ship docked and they walked the plank with hundreds of others. One thing about Nassau, Drake told them, was that tourists would find it hard to get lost. There was a main street, a strip with a few minor streets that dissected it, a big market, and a herd of taxis that took you to the impressive but aging Atlantis hotel and back.

"Follow the pack," Ben shouted with a swing in his step.

Drake gave him a little sidelong glance. "Good night?"

Ben opened his mouth to speak but then his mobile rang. "Karin?"

"Hope that didn't interrupt you too much last night, my friend."

Drake moved up to walk alongside Mano Kinimaka. The big Hawaiian had kept himself slightly apart since the 'old' friends got back together and Drake didn't want him to feel alienated. Especially since he wanted to keep an eye on him.

"How's it goin', big guy? I know you saw the same things Hayden saw. You handling it any better than she is?"

Kinimaka looked a little shocked. "I was warned you were blunt, but . . ."

"Take me as I was born and bred," Drake shrugged. "As a Yorkshireman."

"We weren't friends, but I feel sorry for them and their families. I hate Boudreau and his boss. I'm in this to the very end, believe me."

"Good." Drake slapped the giant on the back and, for the thousandth time in his life, wondered if every trained soldier sized the other man up for his weak spot even as they were simply chatting.

They took a right down Bay Street, still among the horde, but as the gift shops and restaurants began to grow more plentiful the crowd began to thin. They followed the signs for the Pirates Museum - not that they had to, because when they found the place it was one of the gaudiest buildings Drake had ever seen. Painted in light purple, with a massive depiction of the skull and crossed swords, the museum seemed to offer tack and fake plunder rather than authentic swag.

Kennedy frowned as she eyed the makeshift stocks outside. "This the right place?"

"Aye, me hearty," Drake growled, laughing at their disgusted expressions. Then he sobered. "And on that darker note, keep an eye out, boys and girls. We won't be the only team in town."

"We might be." Ben sounded a little hurt.

"I'm not saying you're crap, mate, just that there might be one or two others out there who measure up to your talents."

They walked into an air-conditioned room, found a guide and beckoned him over. To their surprise he knew immediately what they were looking for.

"There is a small authentic museum out back," he told them. "Tourists are usually too busy with the stocks, eye-patches and dress-up to even notice it's there." The man was old and grey, but virile-looking, as if he still worked out and ate well. "You folk are the third set since yesterday been asking 'bout that ole rag. Not unheard of, but unusual."

"Third set in two days?" Ben shook his head. "I must be losing it."

Drake immediately eyed Kinimaka. The Hawaiian caught on straight away and fell back to scout the surrounds. Who was to say one of the sets hadn't left a welcoming committee?

"Anyway, it's over here," the old man said as he wandered through a pink door with rickety hinges and pointed at an open display case, one of half a dozen in the tiny room. "Thing's chained down, o' course. Trust ain't one of the museum's strong points."

Hayden led the way, striding over to the display case without heed or evaluation. Drake followed a few steps behind, giving Kennedy the same stare as Kinimaka and making sure she understood to check their perimeter.

When he reached the display case he wasn't all that impressed.

A tatty old rag lay before them. Nothing but yellowed and blackened paper, scrawled over in faint spider patterns, the ink worn and washed away.

"That it?" Ben voiced everyone's thoughts.

Hayden reached out to flick the pages. Ben said the obligatory: "Careful." With a few practiced movements she had found the passage they were looking for. Drake took a moment to appraise the room. Kennedy was at the door. The cabinets all around them were dull and dusty, suffering from neglect. The shelves were bowed and creaked every time someone moved. The single row of windows, high up, held a layer of dirt so thick even the Bahaman sun failed to penetrate.

Kennedy nodded that she was satisfied with their perimeter.

Hayden leaned forward to study the writing. "Edward Teach brought forth two boxes, one of shiny and magnificent lustre and one of cheap design. But when joined, imagination would struggle to conjure a more Hell-like image. The very ground did begin to swell and shake and with mine own eyes I did see some folk vanish as if they had never existed." She looked at Ben and Drake. "That's just the first page," she read a few passages to herself. "It seems Blackbeard brought the device to their meeting and demonstrated its power to prove his superiority. Calico Jack invited Blackbeard back to his-" Hayden squinted. "Abode? Does that say abode?"

Ben nudged her aside, eager to get a look. Drake grinned. "Yes," his young friend said. "They retired to Calico Jack's abode and, luckily, our scribe went with them."

Hayden pushed her way back in. "The air between the two Pyrates was charged with a fearful tension. Blackbeard himself set off the fuses beneath his hat, making them fairly crackle and fizz. Jack took great mirth in this, miming the terror and quick flight of his enemies. Blackbeard, his face barely apparent through his magnificent growth, explained to Jack how he was feared there and that a battle was coming. A battle he could not ignore."

"Interesting," Ben nudged again. "My turn."

Hayden suffered him to lean in. Ben refused to speak Pyrate, instead first digesting the text and then reciting it his own way. "Blackbeard arrived at this meeting with Calico Jack hotly pursued by two men-of-war. Now, Teach didn't back down from a fight so he fully intended to take them on, but he wanted Calico Jack to look after the device until he returned." Ben paused. "Now that's one trusting pirate."

"And the reason he demonstrated his power," Drake said. "Best guess - there's a way to make it work that only Blackbeard knew."

"And don't forget Blackbeard's Claw," Kennedy shouted. "Dude sounds like some serious backup."

"So that would make me-" Ben raised a dreamy face, "Drake's Claw."

Hayden pushed him away. "Our Heroe, Captain Teach, the man who scared America more than any other, did charge Calico Jack with the safekeep of his fearsome Storm Maker, and promised to heap gold cups and barrels of wine and many other treasures upon him, but did leave a dire warning-"

"That Calico Jack would vanish from this Earth, leaving no trace of him ever living, if he dared to double-cross Edward Teach," Ben finished with a flourish.

Drake thought about that. "Nasty threat to say the least. I would imagine a pirate like Calico Jack would take heed, bearing in mind the reward of course."

Through the open door, voices drifted. Drake turned to Kennedy. The New Yorker shook her head, miming: "Tourists."

"He did," Ben was reading rapidly now, "Ole Blackbeard went off to fight his battle. The scribe says Jack sent the pieces of the device home for security and pretty much went on with his pirating ways. That was until he was hanged, of course, not long after, in 1720."

Drake frowned at them both. "Is that it?"

Ben pulled a face. "Yeah."

"So the story might continue from Jack's home, or from when Blackbeard returned," Hayden said, stepping down from the dais that surrounded the cabinet. "We don't know of anything on the Blackbeard side," she said looking up at Ben. "In your research did you read anything about Calico owning land? I know several of these pirates were landowners or had wealthy families."

Ben thought back. "Not much was known about Calico - or Jack Rackham - before he became a pirate. Seems you have to be notorious to be famous. I think he was born in Jamaica, though English." Ben blinked and snapped his fingers. "But yes, of course, Anne Bonney was his wife. She became pregnant by him."

Drake saw where he was going. "And what happened between them?"

"Gimme a break, crusty. I can't remember." The young lads' eyes gleamed. "Take me to a computer."

Hayden received a call and headed towards the exit. Drake shrugged at Ben and followed. Outside they met up with Kinimaka and waited on the sun-blasted corner whilst the CIA agent finished.

It didn't take long. With a jab of frustration she turned to them. "Still not one single shred of information leading to the Blood King. The guy's harder to find than a damn ghost." She took a moment to breathe. "Ed Boudreau however, is extremely well known. High on the watch lists, even higher on the wanted lists. The world and its dog wanna hump this guy's leg all the way to jail."

"Mercenary? Ex-military?" Drake guessed.

"Most of them are as you know. Boudreau appears to have one extra thing going for him though - his connections. For some reason he has his claws into some very powerful organisations."

Drake's own phone sang out an old Dinorock number, specially selected for Ben. School's Out by Alice Cooper.

"Hello?"

"Drake, my friend."

Mai's soft, sensual tones filled his senses once more. Drake steeled himself before answering. "Hello, Mai. Do you have information for me?"

Ben turned to stare. Kennedy raised an eyebrow, privy only to the smallest details of the Japanese superspy, but aware much more was hidden away.

"I have concluded my business in San Francisco. My government want me to take an interest in the Blood King conspiracy. Various American arses are currently being . . . greased? I told them I might join a team that was already on the ground."

"Us?" Drake blurted before he could stop himself. "You want to join us?"

"Could you handle it?" The barest suggestion of laughter.

Drake coughed to gain a little time. The question was accurate and fully loaded. Could he? Mai Kitano – codename Shiranu in tribute to some deadly video game character who was big in Japan - was a fantastic operative; a woman who never failed to get what she wanted. An advantage that could sometimes turn certain things into a huge problem.

"I guess we could use you."

"Ah, there's the sweet talking Drake I know. I'm heading over to Miami on the next flight out. Call you when I land."

The connection went dead. Drake let out a deep breath and gestured wildly. "Let's go find a damn computer."

*****

"Calico Jack and Anne Bonny did have a child together. Born in Cuba, it was quickly taken to sea. It started its life in battle as Jack attacked several Dutch merchant vessels . . ." Ben paused, reading on. The others were all stood around him like a team of bodyguards, taking up most of the tiny cafe on Marlborough Street.

"Child's not spoken of again for some time. When Calico Jack was captured, Anne Bonney spoke at his trial, saying the immortal line - if he had fought like a man, he need not be hanged like a dog.'" Ben whistled. "Nice woman."

"Be warned . . ." Hayden said with half a smile.

"After the trial Bonnet claimed to be pregnant, an act which gave her a stay of execution. Her trial was halted and then . . . then she was spared execution."

"So they had two kids?" Kinimaka was frowning as if all the information hurt his brain.

"The trial was in Jamaica," Ben lectured. "If Bonney was pregnant then she probably settled there."

"You said Calico Jack was born in Jamaica," Drake said. "Ironic that he was hanged there too. But what if Bonney - the lonely, pregnant widow - was taken in by Rackham's old family and brought her two kids up in his old house?"

"Makes sense." Ben nodded. "And the historical records should be right here."

Drake slapped his friend's shoulders. "Were Bad to the Bone, matey. Bad to the Bone."

CHAPTER EIGHTEEN

The Blood King, man, myth and psychotic killer, stood at the prow of his boat, gazing out to sea. The sun was fading in the sky, sinking low towards the far mountains, and it was that time of day when he felt the need and the deep desire to preserve his reputation.

His men were well versed. They nodded respectfully at the mere flick of his head and scurried off to initiate the most terrible deed of the day.

On this quiet day, at least.

The Blood King took a few minutes to survey his kingdom. And it was a vast, sumptuous kingdom. Six hundred feet and fifteen thousand gross tons. An early-warning system. Laser shields. Armour plating. Helicopter hangar. Submarine dock. The list went on to the tune of $800 million.

But no matter. There was no record of the Stormbringer ever being commissioned, let alone constructed. No matter, its on-board mini-sub and tenders allowed the 'crew' access and egress without danger of being spotted, and its tendency to keep to unused waters kept its visibility low key. Even if it was seen in the occasional harbour, its outside was designed to look like a Super Yacht's charter, something the mega-rich of Monaco or Dubai might rent for a few months at a time.

Occasionally he lost track of exactly who was on his ship. He employed a small army, literally, and a crew of hundreds. But again, no matter, he employed people he trusted to look after the banality of everyday life.

He pursued other interests.

Like now, for instance.

His men were dragging a half-starved Ukranian up from below decks. The Blood King let his lip curl in distaste. The prisoner wore little apart from tattered boxer shorts and a stinking blanket of filth. After so many days of imprisonment he'd lost the will to scream. All hope of escape or reprieve had well and truly deserted him.

The Blood King liked seeing desperation in a man's eyes. The thrill came when his captive finally understood he was about to die. After that it was the gloating, and then moments of pleasure when the Blood King watched the man's blood wash across his shoes.

The Blood King lifted an eyebrow. A lackey brought today's weapon of choice - a good old-fashioned broadsword. No doubt priceless. No doubt ancient. But still something that would rest at the bottom of the ocean in about ten minutes.

"Here." He drew an imaginary line with the point of the sword. His men dragged the prisoner forward, carefully placing his knees exactly where the Blood King demanded.

Voice deep and rough, accent unblemished from untold years of being away from his mother country, the Blood King asked the prisoner if he had had a good life; if he missed his family, his children. If he hoped one day to see them again, in heaven.

The blank, broken look turned immediately into recollection and regret. Into hope. A momentary spirit galvanised the prisoner and he started to have thoughts about moving. Then the Blood King severed his dirty head from his dirty shoulders and he thought no more.

Thick blood washed the decks.

"One a day, every day, forever," the Blood King grunted. "Tomorrow we will spin the Vodka bottle again. Let some of them have their hope."

He turned to study the far, purple mountains, the dead man and the horrendous deed already forgotten. "It will be but brief."

CHAPTER NINETEEN

The flight from Nassau to Kingston, Jamaica, took a couple of hours. Upon landing Drake received a call from Wells. The SAS commander had no new information whatsoever and Drake found himself wondering if the guy was fishing.

"Look, sir," he found it hard to give up old habits, "either you've been told to pump me for information or you've heard something and want in. Either way, just ask."

"You know I keep tabs on the Japanese chatter," Wells admitted, then went quiet.

Drake sighed. "Yes, she's coming." He filed with the others into passport control. "Look, I'm going to have to go now. I guess I'll be seeing you soon?"

"Just try to keep me away." And the line went dead, leaving Drake wondering how, with all this amazing technology around, the great secret of the Blood King still remained.

Half an hour later and they were well on their way through Kingston, seated inside a rumbling, bouncing van. Like the reggae vans of Barbados, this thing was ancient, colourful and extremely noisy. Bob Marley tunes blasted from the music box. The only difference was they were alone on this journey, instead of being crammed in with forty other people on a fifteen-seater ride.

The place they were looking for was called Stony Hill, now part of a warren of roads and housing on the edge of a no-man's-land. The man they were looking for was Lionel Raychim, an engineer now retired, responsible for several of Jamaica's main roads that formed the backbone of the island's transport system.

Rick's Bar was located in a grubby corner of a cul-de-sac, a ramshackle place surrounded by stone buildings, the very focus of the sun's baking heat.

Drake paid the driver and headed for a door covered by American beer signs. Budweiser. Coors. Michelob. "Don't worry," he said, laying a consoling hand around Ben's shoulders, "we'll get you a glass of icy cold milk."

Rick's Bar was surprisingly agreeable once the heat and the location were fastened away behind them. The meandering, dimly lit place was wood-panelled and decorated with a mind-boggling array of furnishings: from a pirate cutlass to a Jolly Roger flag that hung next to the green and black Jamaican flag, and from the often replicated picture of workers sitting along the girders of the Empire State Building, to standard bikini babes posing on an idyllic beach. Drake smiled. It was easy to imagine ole Rick tacking stuff on the walls here and there, anything he could get his hands on. The place smelled of beer, sweat and cooking meat.

A family of English tourists, their legs and arms the colour of virgin paper, were finishing off a meal, not looking at their food but studying the locals as carefully and warily as they could. A drunk sat at the bar, head slumped and hair dangling in his own dinner.

"Awesome," Kennedy shook her head. "Let's find Raychim and get back to civilisation."

"This ain't so bad," said Hayden looking a little hurt. "Small town girl - I grew up in a place with a bar like this. We can't all have a Denny's on the doorstep you know."

Kinimaka walked slap bang into a table, spilling a guy's drink and waking up the drunk at the bar. The Hawaiian said: "Oops, sorry," and skirted around, going red.

"If that'd been me," Ben commented, "there'd have been threats, fist shaking, maybe even a head-butt."

Drake glanced at him. "Not while I'm here, there wouldn't."

They found a table and sat down, Kinimaka looking especially uncomfortable perched on an undersized chair. A waitress with jet-black curly hair and a dirty pinny came out from the back, spotted them, and hurried over.

"Help you?" Her English was stilted and tuneful,

but a million times better than any of their Jamaican.

"I hope so," Kennedy took the lead. "We're looking for Buds, all round, and a chat with Lionel Raychim."

The waitress instantly looked suspicious. "Wha' you need wit' old man Ray?"

"A history lesson," said Kennedy laying some cash on the table. "He around today?"

"Whoever y'ask prob'ly tol' you he 'round every day," said the waitress studying them hard before seeming to come to a decision. "Jus' wait."

She went to the bar, took her pinny off, then turned and disappeared around the side into another room. Drake surveyed the place, catching the eyes of Kennedy, Hayden and Kinimaka. They got the message, each abruptly sitting lighter and weighing their options.

Around the corner came a tall, spare man with white hair, a white beard and wearing a white suit. Oddly, he still looked more tanned than the English family who gawped at him and surreptitiously reached for camera phones. Upon reaching their table he sat down, spirited the money away and shouted loudly for beer.

His eyes met Drake's. "What do you need?"

Kennedy spoke first, butting in with such vigour that her unshod hair whipped forward. "We believe you might be the descendant of a pirate called Calico

Jack. His only descendant. And that you still own the farm where his family were brought up." Out loud it actually sounded ludicrous, though their research was sound.

Raychim glared at them. The waitress made a reappearance, bringing them their Buds and sliding Ben's across with a little wink. Drake grinned.

"Alcohol, not milk? Wasn't that a song?"

"Dr Feelgood." Ben studied the Bud. "We covered it. The band, I mean."

Kennedy gave Raychim a little push. "Are you that man, Mr Raychim?"

The man's eyes flicked from left to right. "You eating?"

Drake took a closer look. Lionel Raychim's hands were shaking, just a little. His nose was a red network of broken veins. His tongue flicked nervously across his lips. The man was a drunk, and probably didn't eat much. "Choose what you want," Drake said. "Just do us a favour - talk whilst you eat. We don't have a lot of time."

Raychim nodded and ordered the biggest steak and chips dinner on the menu with all the trimmings, and more Bud besides. "I still own that farm, though I hadn't been there in over five years."

Kennedy leaned forward. "Hadn't?" Drake couldn't help but watch her long black hair fall this way and that.

"There was a break-in two days ago. Many books were taken."

"What kind of books?"

"Old ones. The kind of thing that might pertain to my ancestor, the famous pirate."

Drake had been thinking: two days? They were really that far behind their rivals? Then Raychim's words jolted him.

"They took the books?"

"Hmm," Raychim became distracted as his food arrived. Kinimaka had ordered a burger. No one else dared the local fare.

"Most of them."

Kennedy bit. "You saying they didn't get what they wanted? Do you think that something in these books might be helpful to them?"

"So many questions," Raychim drained half his first Bud, using his napkin to hold the glass and wiping his mouth on a white sleeve.

"Not everything." Raychim put his knife and fork down and grinned. "I may be old, I may be a drunk. I may be a lot of things, but I ain't stupid. I knew, as soon as that cursed old box was dragged up on prime-time TV that people would come sniffing. You ain't the first, won't be the last."

Hayden placed her arms on the table." But we are the most official." She flashed her credentials.

Raychim looked relieved. "It's a book they are looking for," he said immediately. "I have it in my car."

*****

Not surprisingly, Raychim's car was parked outside. Within ten minutes, Ben was thumbing carefully through the pages of the antiquated book. "Yes," he exclaimed, "this is the scribe's continuation piece. You know . . . " he mused, " . . . this book might be worth a fortune if offered in the right circles."

"Not now," Drake chastised the youngster. "Speak, or the dummy goes back in."

"The scribe wrote that after Blackbeard's battle had finished the pirate could not return to Calico Jack. It doesn't say why . . ." Ben scanned forward for answers. "No, nothing. Maybe the Queen Anne's Revenge was damaged?"

Drake nodded. "Or being pursued. There were a lot of British men-of-war around here at the time tasked with ridding the seas of pirates."

"Whatever," said Kennedy tapping the table. "What happened next?"

"Blackbeard got word to Calico Jack and ordered him to send the devices to a prearranged meeting place. Look. There's a map here, and even an X. A real pirate treasure map!" Ben's excitement made his eyes wide and glassy.

To a person, everyone stood up and craned over to take a look. The revered silence that followed was a testament to notorious pirate history.

Ben continued. "It seems that Calico Jack did send the devices to the agreed meeting place on a small ship, or boat. It's not clear. But the boat was intercepted by the British, its crew killed and its valuables confiscated."

"So the British claimed the devices?" Hayden wondered.

"Yes. Blackbeard never collected them, in any event. Maybe he sent a scouting party to the rendezvous point and they saw what happened." Ben read on for a few minutes and then closed the book.

Hayden glared at him. "Well?"

"That's it."

"That's it? What the hell-"

"There are a few passages about how Jack shipped his own treasures home and ordered them to be stowed away in his cellar for when he later returned. Of course, he never did."

"So the British took the devices-" Drake pulled a face as he chewed the information over in his brain. "Damn the Limeys."

"And the rusty box ended up on Blackbeard's ship," Kinimaka said, moving slightly and making the whole right side of the pub shudder. "At the bottom of the ocean."

"But that's because the British killed him and sunk the Queen Anne's Revenge."

Lionel Raychim was switching between eating noisily and slurping Bud like his life depended on it. The Jamaican waitress kept close watch from behind the bar. Every time Raychim drained a bottle she came skipping over with another. Maybe she was Rick and she owned the damn place.

"Wait," Ben said so slowly Drake could almost hear the gears grinding. "Wasn't Blackbeard offered a pardon by the British?"

"Yeah," Kennedy drawled. "And he accepted it, according to the Web. Didn't stay chained to his masters for long though."

"Exactly," Ben said. "He accepted the pardon, got himself to wherever they were keeping the box - or device - and promptly escaped with it."

"Only to be caught and killed by that Maynard guy, his ship sunk on the spot." Drake ran through what he remembered. "Doesn't explain why they only found the rusty box though and not the clock, controller-thing."

"Maybe the British kept it," Kinimaka suggested.

"I doubt that," Drake mused. "Not judging by what we know of Blackbeard. If that controller was there, you can bet your bollocks he'd have taken it."

"And if it wasn't?" Kinimaka looked confused.

"Then good ole Calico Jack - this man's esteemed ancestor," Drake clapped Lionel Raychim on the back, spraying Bud and bits of steak everywhere, "did the one thing we would never have expected of anyone. He double-crossed Blackbeard."

CHAPTER TWENTY

Kennedy twisted around in her chair, shuffling and tugging at her jeans as she did so. Drake saw Raychim take a quick gander towards the offending area before looking away with a guilty expression.

"Don't sweat it, old man. Ass cracks are in this year," he paused . . . "or out, depending on your point of view. Lol."

Kennedy sent him a mock glare. "Dick. You don't say lol. You spell it out in an email or something."

Hayden was running a hand through her blonde hair, looking tired and overwhelmed. "Jack double-crossed Blackbeard? How?"

"Simple. He just sent the crappy box back to the rendezvous and then somehow alerted the British about the drop-off. His plan's only failure occurred when Blackbeard himself didn't turn up. That problem was negated later, though, when the pirate accepted his pardon."

"That means Blackbeard wouldn't have known about Jack's double-cross until the moment he found the box in the British stronghold."

"Yes," Ben was on a roll, "and then, of course, he ran off and got dead."

"Taking the 'hard-drive' to the bottom of the sea," said Drake nodding his head, "where it lay, randomly emitting displacement waves whenever a chain of events set it off, until the salvage team brought it up."

"Like in Lost." Kinimaka mentioned a series close to his heart and his actual home.

"Which could be anything," Hayden said, talking over her colleague. "From sea-bottom earthquakes to crazy currents to-"

"A stroke from a mermaid?" Drake's soldiers mind couldn't help it.

Kennedy sat back a bit self-consciously. "That takes care of the box. But what about the controller? What did Jack do with that?"

Raychim slurped down more beer.

"He kept it," Kinimaka said unnecessarily.

But that simple sentence made Ben sit up. "Of course he did! He ordered all his treasures shipped home and stored away in his cellar. Remember?"

All eyes turned to Raychim. The man in white finished off yet another Bud, wiped grease from his cheeks, and smiled for the first time. "Wondered when you'd catch up."

*****

Hayden rounded on him in an instant. "Sir, this is an official investigation. We're on a deadline here. If you have-"

"Calm down, calm down. Keep yer frillies on," the old man laughed. "I wouldn't have gotten fed and watered if I gave it up in the first place. Good lesson for you there, young lady," he cackled. "Any case - I don't have Calico Jack's treasure. The whole shebang was donated to a museum about ten years ago. Famous one, too."

Drake looked at Ben and Kennedy thinking for God's sake don't say the Louvre. They hadn't yet repaired it properly since their last little visit.

"It was all donated to the Key West Museum of Art and History. I remember it, too. Shaped like an hourglass with brass arms that I'm guessing now are what attach it to this box of yours. Fancy thing. Classic pirate swag."

"Key West?" Drake looked around at his friends. "End of the line in more ways than one."

Mano Kinimaka looked thoughtful. "Isn't there a Hard Rock Cafe there?"

*****

Drake pushed out the door first into the blinding sun. Despite the glare his eyes fell immediately on the trio of men standing around Lionel Raychim's car. One of them was bent over by the passenger-side door, the other two were watching. Were they working for the council?

Without a word Drake signalled the others and took off at a sprint. By the time the men looked up he was among them. They were untrained, probably local muscle who'd never come up against a trained soldier before.

By the time Hayden and Kennedy arrived Drake stood over two writhing bodies and had the third pinned by his neck against the car.

"What are you doing?" he shouted as the man struggled. Drake slammed him back against the car. "No! What the hell are you doing?"

"Just . . . looking," the Jamaican wheezed. "We didn't know it was yours."

"It's not." Drake looked around, assessing the situation. If these guys were locals tasked by an unknown to steal Raychim's car then they would know nothing. They weren't even worth beating up. He kicked a few ribs and threw the man to the ground, careful to keep an eye out for weapons.

"Get the hell out of here."

All the time he searched their surroundings. Empty windows stared back at him from up high. Cluttered gardens and dishevelled yards stood on three sides, a kind of barren no-man's-land to the north-east. If they were anywhere, they were in there.

"Something's there . . ." Kennedy said as she quested around. "Can't actually see a damn thing though."

Drake shared her unease. Once you'd served a stretch in the 22 Regiment with the SAS you tended to develop extra senses even faster than a three-year-old wants to grow up.

"I get the feeling we're being watched," Drake agreed. "But, by Christ, if we are - they're good."

"Boudreau?" Hayden's discomfort showed in her voice.

"Wouldn't he come out spitting blood?" Drake said. "No. By someone more subtle, someone with a different game to play." He made a snap decision. "Let's go. Hayden, . . . you need to make a call. Get Mr Raychim here some protection."

Hayden nodded at Kinimaka. "Do it."

Drake smiled at Raychim. "Better put those keys away, pal. You're not driving. Now where's the airport?"

CHAPTER TWENTY-ONE

Hayden pulled some strings and their plane was in the air within an hour. A special charter, it did a fair bit of clunking down the runway, making even Drake grip the armrests with more disquiet than usual at take-off.

It would be a short flight. They toyed with the idea of alerting the local authorities, of even sending in the marines, but decided a small incursion would work better, especially since they were betting that no one else had followed the clues this far. Nevertheless, Hayden alerted her boss, Jonathan Gates, who was aware of the security breaches during the last few days.

His words, to her, left them in no doubt as to the seriousness of what was happening behind closed White House doors. "There is no trust, Hayden. No one to trust. Contact me and me alone."

"There is no trust," Kennedy repeated. "What's going on over there?"

"Nothing to make us lose our focus," Drake said. "The Blood King already holds one of the devices. Chances are, if he gets the second there'll be a few changes in world government."

Ben stared at him as if he'd only just realised the severity of the situation. "Are you kidding?"

Hayden turned on him, trying but failing not to vent her frustrations on her younger boyfriend. "This ain't Call of Duty, Ben. It ain't even a Michael Bay movie. Not yet. It's the kind of thing where people die. People you love and respect and never get back." Her words choked. Drake imagined what she had gone through during the last few days, not to mention the loss of her father to 'the job'.

Drake dropped his eyes as the couple followed their similar routine - regret, makeup, then a few guarded smiles. The Michael Bay dig was probably aimed at Drake. Since the 'Odin thing' Drake had been the focus of attention for many well-known names and corporations, all trying to buy his friendship, his trust, his endorsement, and his name. One big call had been from Bay's management company, with a query as to movie rights.

His mind wandered. He just couldn't get past the feeling of being watched that they had experienced in Jamaica. Even driving to the airport had made the hairs on the nape of his neck crawl and prickle. And now - was it possible to feel as if you were being followed in an aeroplane? He laughed aloud.

The others, tired, tetchy and mentally exhausted, all turned to him. "What are you laughing at, crusty?" Ben asked.

"Just concentrate on the research, Blakey. Key West's an hour away, and we need to be fully prepped." He glanced at each member of the team. "We have to prepare for every eventuality. This is the way I see it . . ."

*****

Whilst Drake talked, Kennedy drifted. It was only now that she was starting to question her motives throughout the last six weeks. Now - when stark reality and another power-crazed dictator had invaded her life through Matt Drake - she wondered if this really was the right place for her. No question, she wanted to be with Drake. But her life had pretty much been put on hold for him.

This is your life, a voice told her. The start. At some point you had to let the torrent of life take you and lie back in its arms, and drift.

Her nature rebelled against that thought. Or was it her confident, New York upbringing? Lindsey Buckingham allegedly wrote the famous words Go Your Own Way when he split up with Stevie Nicks. But it was the next line of the song that always freaked her out. All her life she had felt a singular loneliness, in school, in the Academy, in the station room, every night of every day.

She didn't feel that with Drake. The guy was larger-than-life and more than enough to keep her engaged twenty-four hours a day.

It actually scared her to think she might have found all that she was looking for. Here, with these people - Drake, Ben, Hayden in particular and even Mano Kinimaka whose heart of gold was already winning her over - was where she wanted to stay.

She was sure of it. Almost.

Drake had paused to stare at her, bringing her back to the present. "You ready?"

"Sorry?"

"Plane's about to land. We're here."

CHAPTER TWENTY-TWO

Key West was an outstanding anomaly. Full of seaside bustle and commercialism, it still managed to capture that feeling of American originality, wealth and old pirate secrets all wrapped up in a palm tree-enclosed, laid back paradise. Huge pelicans followed fishermen around as if on a leash and dived for the fish they might have caught with good-natured squawks. The balmy weather brought the tourists flocking and the main thoroughfare, Duval Street, was overrun with day-trippers and holiday-makers, and bustling with a carnival-like atmosphere.

The five most unlikely treasure-hunters of them all picked their way through the happy chaos, heading for the ocean. Already they could see the clear blue sea glistening at the bottom of Duval Street.

"One thing's for sure," Drake muttered. "Anyone following us down here sure won't have to work too hard."

Kinimama was examining every side street, every bar.

Kennedy said, "You're trying too hard, big dude. Tone it down a bit. The bad guys're gonna find it hard to miss you anyway."

"Bad guys?" Kinimaka grunted. "I'm looking for the Hard Rock."

Drake headed left, bypassing the path them led to the ocean overlook where the big ships were normally moored. He paused, pretending to take a breather against some railings, whilst Ben studied the map. Drake surveyed their flanks.

Nothing. Not a glimmer out of place nor a flicker to worry about. Should there be? It didn't matter. He felt responsible for them all now. He would cover their backs and worry twice as much as he probably needed to.

He wondered briefly why Wells hadn't called yet. Why Mai hadn't been in touch. But then Ben pointed to the left and they began to thread through the tourists again. Music drifted from a nearby bar. Laughter rode the summer air like a blessing. These people didn't need to know about a myth called the Blood King.

Five minutes later and they were standing outside the Museum of Art and History. Drake turned to Ben. "Tourists?"

Hayden clicked at them impatiently. "CIA," she said impatiently, then relented and added "Bitches," for effect.

Kennedy pushed ahead of them all. "Feel like I've got a damn target on my back," she grumbled and disappeared inside. Drake, for all his vigilance, felt the same and waved everyone on ahead before taking a last look around, and then following.

*****

She hadn't seen Drake in a while. He hadn't changed. Neither had that bitch, Kennedy Moore. And they still had the kid, Ben Blake, nipping at their heels. The CIA agent she'd encountered - and playfully kissed several times back when they first captured her in Sweden - looked like she needed a major banging to bring those stress levels down a bit, and was being almost as vigilant as Drake.

And the big guy? Now he looked interesting.

She'd followed them carefully, cleverly, all the way from Jamaica. Lionel Raychim had long been a player on Boudreau's list, and when Boudreau learned of Alicia's long history with Drake, it only seemed right to send her after the ex-SAS man.

Alicia Myles turned to her own big buy, the techno-wonder known as Tim Hudson. "Huddo," she whispered her own private nickname for him. "Keep behind me, big boy. Drakey ain't gonna like us turning up uninvited like this. The boys . . . " she rolled her eyes to the left, " . . . need to be taken in by the act, too."

"I know the plan, Alicia." Hudson was clearly dying for a smoke, but now wasn't exactly the time.

"Give 'em about ten minutes inside," Alicia said, checking her watch. "Then we'll move."

*****

Inside, the museum was cool and quiet. A few people milled about the entryway and amongst the cabinets and display cases beyond. Drake scrutinised all of them, but nothing made his sixth sense prickle.

Hayden decided to forgo all the treasure-hunt business and presented her credentials at the counter. The young woman behind the desk stared at them blankly.

"Yes?"

"CIA."

"I can see that, Miss. Congratulations."

"Don't get smart. Just point us towards the Calico Jack donations."

"I wouldn't work in a museum if I were smart, Miss, I'd work in a library. It's that way." She jerked a thumb through a nearby door and went back to her work.

Drake stared at Hayden and Hayden stared at the woman. They couldn't quite tell if she'd just been insulted. Was that the point?

"Onward," said Ben now leading the way. Drake reflected on the last few museums he'd visited. Things hadn't really worked out too well for the owners.

The Calico Jack exhibition was surprisingly large. Row upon row of small and sparkly artefacts sitting upon numerous shelves, each one tagged accordingly. To their credit the museum clearly looked after its donations. Every item of pirate booty gleamed or sparkled.

The controller was easy to spot. By far the largest item in the exhibit, it had been placed at the back but still managed to dominate. The body was shaped like a slender hour-glass and marked all over with arcane symbols, the like of which would undoubtedly make some archaeologists day. Attached to the top of the hour-glass and sweeping down the body in a gentle curve were the 'arms'. These were made of some kind of hard metal that shimmered under the pinpoint lights of the display. The 'arms' ended in a kind of pincer, like a crab's claw, that were clearly intended to attach to something.

The dull, supposedly worthless, box. The hard-drive.

Drake made sure Kinimaka and Kennedy were happy with their perimeter. "Ok. So, Hayden, you gonna break the glass or do we go official?"

Hayden gave him a sharp glance. "What do you have against museums, Drake? We give Gates a call, of course.

The CIA agent wandered off, clicking buttons. Drake had to wonder briefly why some people always walked around when talking on their cell-phones. Maybe that was why some countries called them 'mobile'.

He surveyed the team, and then took a moment to laugh at himself. What was he doing? He wasn't a solider any more, wasn't even half a soldier, judging by the way Alicia Myles had kicked him all over the floor of that chateau in Germany. Problem was, the desire had faded away faster than the name of today's blockbusting movie-star. Now, he was a man who had lost something, and a man who knew the name of the baby he could never have with his dead wife.

Emily. They would have called her Emily. Alyson had been four months pregnant when she died. Their final argument, one of many since Drake learned of the impending baby and struggled to come to terms with it, had already convinced him that he wouldn't let either of them go ever again, even as Alyson walked out the door.

But he let her go that last time. To let her calm down. After a while he would have called her, made it better, made it right forever.

His eyes met Kennedy's and he knew from her expression that her thoughts were as haunted as his own. Kennedy Moore shared the same darkness of extreme repressed memory.

He shook it off. Kennedy turned away. Sooner or later they were going to have to come to terms with their demons.

Kinimaka saw their exchange, but pretended to be studying a row of Spanish cutlasses. A big man with a good heart. Drake opened his mouth to say something but then Hayden came over at a clip.

"Looks like we're sorted here. Cat woman outside should be getting the call from the museum's directors any minute. Once we have it-"

Drake nodded. "We need to move fast, back to Miami."

"That's it," Hayden looked around at the sound of footsteps. "Hey, you alright there, sweetie?"

The woman shot Hayden a look sharper than razor wire. "Please look after the exhibit. You have no idea what it's worth."

"You think?" Hayden started to walk purposefully towards her, face ablaze. She knew what it was worth alright. She knew what it had cost so far.

Ben stood in here way. "Not worth it, love," he said gently. "Not worth it at all."

Hayden stopped, looking amazed. By the time she recovered the museum curator had removed the controller from its place and was ready to hand it over.

Kennedy walked forward, but the woman shied away. "I was told to give it to Miss CIA here, no one else."

Hayden strode forward and grabbed the article. With a massive effort she turned away and nodded to the others. "Let's get out of here."

Drake and Kinimaka led the way, careful to check the foyer area first. There was no one milling around but a pair of old tourists. Drake headed for the exit doors and stepped through.

And time suddenly stood still. His breath literally froze in his throat.

For there, right smack-bang in front of him, holding a nasty-looking Ingram M6 with the military config. and with an evil grin on her flawless face, was the woman who still disturbed his dreams.

Alicia Myles.

CHAPTER TWENTY-THREE

Instantly Kinimaka, Kennedy and Hayden fanned out to the sides. Alicia stayed where she was, eyeing the controller. Drake took a second to appraise the man who stood beside her, a slightly overweight bruiser with a tangled beard. The guy looked familiar.

Then Alicia broke the ice. "Hey boys! Like the look of yer pirate booty there. And speaking of booty," her eyes flicked scornfully at Kennedy. "You still banging that serial killer's bitch, Drake? American ass ride the waves better, does it?" She mimed a few air-spanks.

Drake's eyes were on the gun. Ingram's weren't the best in the world, but at this range even the bearded tit beside her could probably take out half their team.

The tension rose. Drake cast a glance behind her. "Got a crew out there, Myles?"

Without giving her chance he stepped quickly towards her partner. Alicia's eyes immediately lost their confident lustre. "That's what we're here about, Drakey. Hudson and I want to swop sides," she paused. "Now."

That was where he knew the guy from. He had been Abel Frey's techno-wizard. Two months, and she was still with him. The look on her face gave him pause. "So you and the bearded tit want to join us? Why?"

Alicia moved closer to Hudson, Drake noticed, without even realising it. "My boss works for a bloody megalomaniac, Drake. I'll explain in detail later, but I want to stick with you. As for now . . . we don't have a lot of time. Peaches and cream here-" she indicated Hayden and Kennedy. "Need to put on some kind of show."

"A show?" Mano Kinimaka stepped back. "I don't think that's appro-"

"Not that kind of show, dumbo," Alicia snapped. "A show of arresting me, of carting us off. We need to get our ball-sacks out of here now."

Kinimaka grunted. Drake pinpointed several movements behind Myles. "Lot of shooters out there," he said. "How'd you find us? Ah! You were in Jamaica, am I right? You were watching Raychim."

"Tamed and clever." Alicia sent sly eyes at Kennedy. "Can you handle a man who doesn't kill innocent women for a living?"

Kennedy leapt forward. Alicia grinned like her plan was in motion. With a fluid movement any wild Jaguar would have been proud of she twisted out of Kennedy's reach, threw her spare weapon to Drake, and turned and started firing.

The Ingram fired loud. The streets of Key West came to a halt as people stopped what they were doing and turned an ear to the skies. What could that be? Not gunfire? Not here-

Drake shoved Ben around the side of the museum. Hayden drew her weapon, as did Kinimaka. Kennedy stayed with Ben. Drake fired as men emerged from cover about thirty feet away. Two came from behind a toilet block, running hard. Drake dropped them with two quick squeezes of the compact trigger.

Alicia was shooting on full-auto, but then she knew where her former comrades were hiding. Tourists and locals were scattering round the edges, jumping over fences and routing each other across the nearest hotel grounds.

Drake backed away. "Myles! Come on!" He knelt by the corner of the museum, his friends around him, and picked off every man who showed any part of his body. "Damn, we need a way out of this."

"Got that right," Alicia said as she scrambled next to him, Hudson in tow. "There are about thirty of 'em out there."

"Thirty?" Hayden looked horrified.

"Boudreau says his boss always goes over the top. Makes him look hard or whacko or something. Oh, they've got a helicopter too."

"So you do work for Boudreau," Hayden hissed at her. "How can you work for that maniac, you fucked up bitch?"

"Steady," Alicia said without a flicker of concern. "That kind of talk may make me want to kiss you. Again."

Bullets strafed the side of the wall next to them. Drake ducked as brick dust blasted past his eyes. "This way."

Walking backwards, they cleared the museum and ran. Drake turned towards a hail of gunfire that

David Leadbeater

clattered amongst nearby palm trees, but held fire, not wanting to exhaust the clip so early. Then they were suddenly on Duval Street, the thoroughfare still crammed with shoppers and tourists.

"We can't go this way." Hayden shot off to the left, heading towards the ocean and a narrow path. Kinimaka and Kennedy raced after her without pause.

Drake glanced around. At that moment a horde of bad guys came sprinting around the other side of the museum and aimed their weapons down Duval Street.

Hayden and the others were already out of sight.

Drake went the only he could. Into the crowd.

*****

Kennedy sprinted in Kinimaka's wake, not realising she was the last person until Hayden began to slow. When Kinimaka's grunts lost some tempo she glanced back.

"Wait!"

Hayden stopped. "Damn! Where did they get to?"

The tree-lined pathway curved both ways, offering no clear view either forward or back.

"We have to help them." Kennedy made a move.

"No! We must keep going." Hayden still clutched the controller tight to her chest. "Drake can fight off an army if needs be. We must get this device to safety. The Blood King can never get both!"

148

"So he's real again now," Kinimaka was muttering. "Real. Myth. Real. Myth. Hard to keep up."

Hayden set off again, this time with her gun poised and the artefact held more securely. Kennedy reluctantly stayed with them, trusting that Drake along with Alicia Myles as back-up knew how to win a war.

Behind them, gunfire erupted.

*****

Drake blended with the crowd as best he could, pushing Ben before him and trusting Alicia to do her bit for Hudson. They moved up Duval Street, past the small cafes and bars, flitting from group to group and putting as much distance between themselves and their pursuers as they could.

Drake spotted them intermittently. Several were talking into wrist mics and clicking Bluetooth ear receivers. Instructions were being sought.

What worried Drake was the Blood King's reputation. What had probably been a good move on any other day and with any other enemy could well backfire on him today. Hudson was already labouring, he noticed. That kid needed to lay off the bacon butties and stick to lettuce for a while.

The sudden sound of a machine-gun's rattle brought him up short.

The mad bastards were sprinting up Duval Street, machine-guns shouldered, firing as they ran.

Drake did the only thing he could. Dragging Ben and screaming at Alicia to follow, he cut left and pounded straight through the grounds of a restaurant. Slamming people aside, he charged through the front door.

*****

Hayden forced them on by sheer will power alone. Even then it was only when Kennedy heard sounds of pursuit coming along their own path that she put a spurt on. With the bad guys just behind they broke free of the palm-tree lined path and emerged onto a sun-drenched causeway. High concrete embankments were fashioned to form a docking area, running up to the wide road with every manner of boat imaginable tied up to either side. The causeway was their only way forward, yet it offered no concealment.

Hayden kept on repeating the old Jaye doctrine over and over in her head. Survive another minute. Survive just another minute.

When she glanced back again she saw the lead pursuers break clear of the trees. She dropped to her knees and quickly fired off three shots. The men went down in a tangle, catching the legs of those behind them. Mayhem ensued.

Kennedy had sprinted on ahead and now turned, squinting in the bright sunshine. "Boat's the only way off here. Any preferences?"

"One that's already running." Kinimaka barrelled past her and almost bounced off the causeway, landing on the deck of a big white speedboat that lay at rest, burbling in its own gentle wake. Its owners started around in alarm at the big man and then grew even more upset when he waved his gun at them.

"Off."

Without hesitation they dived into the clear, rippling water.

"Nice day for a swim anyway," Kinimaka muttered as Kennedy came to his shoulder.

Hayden landed feet first in the speedboat with shots slamming and skimming off the concrete causeway above her. "Go!"

Kinimaka slammed a huge paw at the throttle. The speedboat responded with a furious roar, taking off faster than a slapper heading backstage at a Kid Rock concert. They threw themselves into the bottom of the boat as machine-gun fire fizzed through the air, less deadly at range than the venomous shouts that were aimed their way.

Hayden put her head up a little and was thankful to see the causeway fading behind. "Keep to the coast!" She shouted at Kinimaka. "We need to call Drake."

And then, behind them, she heard the unmistakable whickering of fast-moving blades.

"Chopper!"

*****

Drake prayed the savages back there had ceased fire when their quarry entered the restaurant. Attacking a CIA safe-house and a military cruiser was one thing – shooting between tourists on one of the busiest streets in Florida was urban warfare.

He raced through the tables, shouting and urging everyone to clear out. Blank looks greeted him at first and a little laughter, until they saw his gun. Then there was a sudden upsurge and a cacophony of screams. But Drake and his colleagues were already through it, the blockage intended to slow their hunters down.

Out through the back door and they were in a small alley. Drake cut left, dragging Ben. A minute later and they were on another street.

An open-topped sports car idled at the kerb before them, its occupant shouting into a mobile phone.

Drake glanced around at Alicia. "That'll do."

*****

Kinimaka pushed the throttle as hard as he dared. Something as powerful as a speedboat could quickly flip and crash in the hands of an inexperienced driver. The chopper soared high into the sky and then angled towards them, men dangling from its open doors with weapons aimed.

The chopper came alongside. Kinimaka turned sharply just as the bad guys opened fire. The boat swerved with a massive plume of water and spray, sending a wave across the helicopter's bows. The machine jerked when the pilot became unsighted and one of the shooters lost his grip and fell screaming into the ocean.

"Hope Blackbeard's waiting down there for you, you asshole," Kinimaka breathed.

The helicopter was swinging around again. Head on, Hayden fired a few shots. Even this close her small revolver struggled to hit the target but she saw at least one of the bullets smash a spider-pattern into the windshield.

But without veering an iota off course the huge machine ploughed on.

This time Kinimaka swerved them underneath the chopper, but the pilot had guessed their strategy. He jerked on the collective, shot the chopper up and over the huge surge of water and dropped it down on the other side.

Good pilot, Hayden thought as she lined his forehead up between her sights and pulled the trigger.

Men's bodies were dangling so far out of the chopper doors that the only way they could stay grounded was by other men hanging on to their ankles. A mighty strafe of machine-gun fire erupted. Hayden felt white heat tangle her hair and pass so close to her temple that it left heat residue on her skin.

She fell back, staring up at the bright sky. It had all almost ended right then. Little blisters of heat still festered on her temple.

But then the chopper dived and headed straight for the speedboat.

*****

Drake kicked out the squawking sports car owner and jumped behind the wheel. Once the others were inside he set off at pace.

Checked the rear view. No bad guys were coming around that corner yet.

Alicia was grinning from ear to ear. "Fucksake Drake!" She shouted. "That sure made me horny. And keeping to the pirate vernacular - want me to walk your plank?"

Hudson laughed along with her, obviously accepting her for what she was. Maybe that was why she liked the bearded geek. And now Drake knew she did like the lad. He had seen her covering him with her body, protecting him, making sure he didn't stray too far. He had never imagined Alicia Myles would fall for a man.

The old Alicia would have been positioning his chunky body in front of her at every turn. And on top of that, he wondered, why had she decided to change sides?

Did she know something about the Blood King?

Drake stepped on the accelerator, weaving in and out of traffic, enjoying the roar of the refined engine. They had outstripped their followers by miles. He found his mobile and tapped the speed dial.

*****

Kennedy heard the phone ring and practically wet herself. Machine-guns had just opened fire. The boats deck had been hit badly, and was taking on water. All they needed at the next pass was for one of the bad guys to grow a brain and aim for the engine.

"What?"

"Alright, love? It's Matt."

"I know. Where are you?"

"Leaving Key West by car. You?"

How the hell could he sound so serene and matter-of-fact? "We're in a goddamn firefight here!" In the background she could hear young Ben chatting to his dad and laughing. Their world seemed a more than a world away.

The chopper was coming in low. Kinimaka had steered the speedboat close to the embankment that led to Highway 1, the overseas highway that linked the Keys to Florida and Miami. They were so close they could see the people in their cars craning over to take a look.

"Are you on Highway 1 yet?"

"Just. Why?"

In the next moment the roar of the chopper drowned out everything except fear and adrenalin and personal well-being. The skids hovered inches from the racing speedboat. Men were now standing on the skids, taking better aim. Hayden picked off two and sent them somersaulting through the turbulence into the sea.

More men stepped out to the slaughter.

Was Boudreau in the chopper? Hayden wondered. Or on the other end of a phone, promising a harsh death to anyone who betrayed him.

Kinimaka threw his gun to Kennedy. He needed to concentrate on keeping them straight. Highway 1 loomed to their right. A bridge was coming up fast. If the speedboat flew under the bridge it might gain them a second or two.

"Three rounds left!" Kinimaka shouted. "Don't waste 'em!"

"Never do." Kennedy took aim and sent another man hurtling to his death. Drake was shouting down the phone now, asking for their position. By the sound he couldn't be that far behind.

Then she saw him to their right. A bright yellow drop-top Hummer with four people somehow crammed inside. She stared.

Jesus, Drake was stood in the passenger side taking aim with Alicia's machine- gun.

Everything else was just a shrieking blur.

All three vehicles rocketed along at breakneck speed. The chopper beside the speedboat, the Hummer on the road beside them, keeping pace. Bullets flew from one to the other. Water and debris from the embankment slewed and sheeted over the bottom of the chopper and the sides of the boat. Kennedy slipped and started rolling around the boat. Hayden picked another bad guy off and then shook her weapon.

"Last one," she flung it aside.

Then the skids of the chopper clipped the speed boat, making the watercraft swing up the embankment. Stones and moss and paper erupted from underneath. The boat hit the water again with a jarring thud but the manoeuvre had hurt them.

The chopper came in again.

In that moment Drake fired his machine-gun. A string of high-powered rounds clattered across the chopper's windshield, stitching a desperate mouth shape into the glass. Blood sprayed around the cockpit and burst out through the bullet holes. The chopper veered up and then down. Men went free-falling from its wide-open doors, screaming all the way to their deaths.

The helicopter came crashing down onto the embankment as the speedboat flashed underneath it. The explosion shook the day apart. Metal and body parts and engine oil burst in every direction.

Kennedy stared at the wreckage they left in their wake. The sudden silence left by the departure of the chopper was almost deafening.

On the road above, Drake was waving at them to slide part-way up the embankment.

"Pull up there!" Hayden directed Kinimaka. "The car will be safer. They don't know how Drake escaped."

"Hopefully," Kennedy mumbled as she began to crawl up the embankment.

In another moment Alicia Myles' grinning face greeted them. "Not bad for a set of Yanks," she shouted through the window. "Get the fuck in then. Let's go!"

CHAPTER TWENTY-FOUR

Headlights cut through the darkness, dead-straight, carving bright columns through the black night.

Key Largo was well behind them. They were approaching the city lights of Miami. Rows and rows of restaurants and gas stations and strip malls opened up on every side. They stopped briefly at a highly efficient Denny's before heading further into the mix of dark and light that was the centre of Miami.

"Fountainbleu?" Ben asked from the back.

"Not this time," Hayden said. "We should work on the assumption that everything is compromised just as our safe-house was. Remember Jonathan's last words: Trust no one. Just me."

"So let's contact Gates first," Drake said. "Tell him what we have. And then find a place to stay. Sound good?"

Hayden nodded. Drake stopped the vehicle and let her out to make the call. Silence reigned around the Hummers' interior for a few minutes. Everyone was either too tired or too mentally blasted to strike up any kind of conversation. Hudson was asleep, snoring like a turbo-charged jack-hammer.

"And this car," Drake said to no one in particular, "needs ditching about an hour ago."

Hayden climbed back in, shaking her head. "Don't know what's got into him. I've never heard him sound so scared," she said, her eyes meeting

Drake's in the crawling dark. She leaned towards him. "He's ordered us to sit tight and wait. Stay hidden. That sound right to you?"

Drake shrugged. "Honestly? Something's been badly off right from the start. If you're asking me I'd say the Blood King has dirt on a lot of highly placed officials and now he's playing the time card until he finds us."

"He will find us," Alicia spoke up from the back seat, unusually subdued. "It's what he does."

"What do you know of him?"

"Very little, I am afraid. But I do have an idea," she said, tugging on Hudson's beard to make him grunt in his sleep. "With this figure of fine health taking the lead."

Drake looked around. "The Bearded Tit? Are you having a laugh?"

"Don't worry. He won't have to leave his desk."

The SatNav showed various hotels in the vicinity. Drake drove until they found a middle-of-the-road place, something with a little class but without any of the tiring arrogance.

The hummer ticked in the midnight stillness, a beast at rest. "Somebody's going to have to drop this thing off somewhere and catch a cab back." Hayden pointed out.

"I'll do it," Kinimaka spoke up immediately. "Always wanted to drive one of these bad boys."

"Well, don't drive it too far," Drake told him. "Ten, fifteen miles. Then get back here."

They climbed out, sore and fatigued. Drake took a moment to stop Hayden. "You got enough cash on you to pay for this?"

"Maybe. If not Alicia here might have to put her mouth to some good use for a change."

"Ooo," Alicia let out a little squeal. "Whatever you like, honey."

"There's always another safe-house, but . . ."

"In these Days Of No Trust? Skip it. That's an old Magnum song, by the way. Blakey here wouldn't even know we were taking the piss out of him. See how kind I can be, munchkin?"

"He means 'no'." Ben twirled a finger around his temple. "It's an age thing."

The foyer was spacious, dominated by a big, stone marble-topped check-in desk. A pretty clerk greeted them as if she'd known them their whole lives.

Drake spoke before Hayden could say a word. "Could we see a floor plan please?"

"The . . . excuse me?"

"I have a condition."

"Oh!" Worked every time. "I guess there's a floor plan over there showing the fire layout."

Drake took a moment. "How's rooms twenty-six to twenty-nine? They free? Failing that, corresponding rooms on any floor above."

Ben whispered: "Stop with the big words, dickhead. You don't know what they mean."

The clerk affirmed that the rooms were free. Drake checked his mobile whilst Hayden sorted the payment out. He'd gotten a couple of texts.

Ironically, one from Wells and one from Mai, both to say they had arrived at Miami International.

"Wait," he motioned to Hayden. "Can you get hold of Kinimaka and ask him to swing by the airport. Backup has arrived."

Kennedy gave him a look. "Anyone in particular?"

"Wells. And Mai."

Ben's neck jerked round so fast his head almost fell off. "Mai? The Mai?"

"You know of her?" Kennedy huffed at him. "Then you know more than I do."

Ben didn't catch the unhappy tone. "I know the legends. A few of them anyway. Drake wouldn't elaborate on the more-" he paused, " . . . dangerous ones."

"Subtle." Drake shook his head. "Look. She's one of the best operatives in the world. We're lucky she's here. And Wells is here too. I don't particularly like the guy but he has some great connections. Deal with it."

"Wells?" Alicia hissed. "I was hoping that old bastard was dead by now."

Drake seemed to remember her having issues with their old commander during the 'Odin thing'. "You threw him down a well, Alicia. Wasn't that enough?"

"Not even close, Drakey."

"What's your problem with Wells anyway?"

But Alicia was already huddling with Hudson. Again it struck Drake as out of character for the careless, violent woman he knew and distrusted. Add to that the fact that both she and Hudson were fugitives. He pigeonholed it for now and started ushering people towards the lifts.

Remembered the layout. Stone desk. Jungle of potted plants to its right. Sofas and a huge fish-tank and a display of fine wines to the left. Three entry doors, one double and revolving, the others single and automatic. A sign that said the stairs were beyond the fish tank. A sturdy drinks dispenser next to the check-in desk. Would they have armed security here? Unknown.

Five minutes later and they were checking their rooms. Drake reconnoitred in his own way and chuckled when he noticed the others doing the same. Only Ben stayed in the middle of the room, taking it all in.

"Cool place."

Drake noticed the adjoining door. Perfect.

"Lines of defence," he said. "This room. Then through the door to the next room. Then-" he pointed out the door to where the corridor dog-legged and finished up against a brick wall. Their other two rooms were at its far end. "Then those two, same principle. Agreed?"

"I'm guessing the fourth and final room has good egress?" Alicia asked carefully.

"Of course, Myles. What do you take me for?"

"Well, my initial reaction is to say a 'fresh, pussy-whipped army dropout with no damn clue what he wants, still living with his long-dead memories. But I could be wrong."

"Fuck you." Drake checked the room for vantage points and places where there might be shelter from bullets. He went and checked the distance from the door to the dog-leg's hallway.

"Only problem I can see with these rooms is they don't offer a decent view of the hotel's entrance."

"Room twenty-nine should," Alicia said sweetly. "Huddo and I will take that one."

"Huddo?" Drake sighed. That woman was an enigma, in some ways still the crazed bitch, in others somewhat mellowed, but she remained one of the most dangerous people he had ever met.

He would never forget that.

Before she walked out the door Alicia turned as if she had forgotten something. "Oh, and CIA girl. Helooo sweetie!"

Hayden looked at her with unreadable eyes.

"Our contribution." She indicated Hudson and herself. "And the vital input that will earn us a pardon."

Hayden sighed. "What could people like you possibly offer the CIA?"

Alicia patted Hudson on the head. "This."

"Tim Hudson's head?"

"Nah, that's my trophy. But what's inside is vital. Hudson was Abel Frey's top computer geek. He's world class. Give him a computer - a good one - with clearance, and he'll find this Blood King arsehole for you in a few days."

"We're the CIA," Hayden said. "We have our own world-class geeks."

"Not like Hudson you don't. Seriously."

"Ok, ok, I'll bite. Why don't we?"

"Hudson doesn't care about you or your boss. He's not motivated by pressure or by being better than the guy in the next cubicle. He already is the next guy. He doesn't care about protocol or government rules. He'll ferret about in there and get down and dirty with the real digital information players. Hackers. Spies. Counterfeiters. And he'll spider-web it right back to the Blood King."

Hayden looked like she might agree. "He can do that?"

"Look at him. Does he look like he spends all day playing football or watching it?"

"Well, it's worth a shot. You can't work from here though. It'll have to be somewhere close by, anonymous. We can't risk the controller device in any way."

Alicia shrugged and turned away. "Plenty of hotels close by, dear. Kiss kiss."

Hayden walked over to the window, giving Ben a weak smile as she passed. Drake slapped the young man's shoulders, preventing him from saying anything soppy or silly.

"Looks like you've been out-geeked, my friend."

"Bah! My band could smash his band to the ground, any day."

Drake laughed. "I bet they could. Any news? You know, on the record deal?"

Ben bit his lip. "Karin reckons the company want the rest of the songs by next month. At this rate the other guys will be sacking me."

"Can't do that, mate. You're the star." Drake was about to elaborate when Kennedy spoke up from her position by the door.

"Kinimaka's back. With friends."

Drake braced himself for the flood of memories.

CHAPTER TWENTY-FIVE

When Mai Kitano walked through the door all eyes turned. Drake held his ground and tried to mask his emotions. That was what Mai would do and, he hoped, was doing now. She came right up to Drake and stopped, a light smile playing around the corners of her lips.

"Been a while, my friend."

"You got that right." Drake enfolded her in his arms for the right amount of time before pushing her away. He could sense eyes burning through the back of his skull. Kennedy's. Ben's. Alicia's.

Mai turned away to greet the others. Drake swallowed hard. The sleek and deadly Japanese woman hadn't changed a bit. Her round baby-face and big black eyes belied any underlying penchant towards violence. The smiles and the lilting laughter were genuine, but fashioned to hide what might lurk beneath the mask.

No doubt now, the most dangerous person in the room was Mai Kitano.

Kinimaka bundled his way inside and saw Ben about to ask Mai a question. "Don't ask," he said. "She's never heard of Ken and Ryu."

"Street Fighter's the other game," Ben hit geek-mode hard. "Mai Shiranui appeared in King of Fighters. Was she really based on you?"

David Leadbeater

"Careful, Blakey," Drake warned. "Do you really think Mai's old enough to have a twenty- year-old video game based on her?"

Ben's mouth suddenly refused to close. "I . . . I . . . ah . . ."

Wells rescued him. The SAS commander had remained unseen until now, standing as he did behind Mano Kinimaka.

"Game first. Nickname later. But I'm just glad to be here." He grinned and then saw Alicia. His face turned white. "What the frig is she doing here? Is she under arrest?"

"She's helping," Alicia told him with a look that could have fried an egg. "I suppose we'll have to see what use an old man of fifty-five can be? Oh, apart from following 'ittle wittle' Mai around."

Alicia grabbed Hudson and left the room, heading for the dog-leg corridor and the room at its far end. Drake trusted her enough to make the reconnoitre herself and report back later.

"Well, it's getting late - or early," he shrugged. "Shall we regroup in a few hours?"

They all took the hint. In a matter of moments he was left alone with Kennedy. The New York cop was eyeing him closely.

"You had a thing with her, yes?"

No reason to lie. "Long time ago. Before Alyson."

"I guessed that. You should have told me."

"Why?"

"Because that's what couples do. Especially when an old flame joins the group."

168

"Ah. Sorry. It all seemed a little awkward." He wondered why women always wanted to know the ins and outs of every little thing.

Kennedy came up close. Her body leaned in to his. Behind her, the open windows looked out onto endless rows of offices, hotel and apartment buildings, all twinkling with their homely lights. The bright beams of car headlights cut sharply through the night.

Kennedy shrugged her trousers down and reached for his. "Now, to coin a time-honoured phrase - 'let's get something straight between us'."

*****

Sometime later, with Kennedy sleeping, Drake swung himself out of bed and went to survey their outskirts. The hotel was twenty-four hour so it wasn't difficult leaving without drawing attention. He swung through a small side door before it had chance to open automatically and stepped into the warm Miami night.

Christ, if only the nights were like this back home instead of the freeze-your-balls-off winters the U.K. usually endured.

The hotel entryway and car park curved around a raised central feature - an extensive rockery, riddled with water fountains and random trees. It was a perfect place to plant a shooter. Or a watcher.

Drake eyed it carefully whilst taking in the rest of the view. Twenty metres down and the occasional car flew along one of Miami's quieter roads. Beyond that were the stark, dirty backs of buildings, rows upon rows of them. An easy place to get lost in.

The road to the right led all the way into the heart of Miami. Drake watched as the cars blasted by, each one inhabited by a soul intent on his destination, aiming towards something, with a life, and a future, and a purpose.

Why didn't he feel the same way?

That one was easy. Because he hadn't resolved Alyson's death. Because he hadn't yet come to terms with losing the child he had never even seen.

A shadow flickered nearby as he had known it would. Mai stepped into the semi-light.

"My friend, I have missed you."

He stared straight ahead, seeing nothing. If the Blood King himself had sauntered up, bristling with weapons, Drake would have see nought but a black haze.

"So much has happened, Mai. Do you remember the last time we were together, in Venice? We didn't have a clue it would be ten years before we saw each other again."

"Yes, I remember. A serial killer called Daniel Belmont. We never caught him. I believe he's still at large."

"Christ. I didn't know that. It's good to see you, Mai."

The Japanese woman gave a demure shrug. "I know."

"I hope Wells didn't give you too much of a hard time."

"He is a pest, for sure. But not someone I can't handle," she said, her tiny mouth twitching as if the idea was laughable. "He is a sex maniac, I think."

"Well, you did get yourself in some . . . shall we say . . . unusual positions, Mai." Drake's own smile was lost in the dark.

"Whenever the operation required it, of course. I serve my country, Drake, by any means. And I get the job done. Did I ever fail?"

"Not that I recall."

"And the record remains the same." She paused. "Is that wrong?"

"It's the song remains the same. Led Zepp." They had come up with the Dinorock banter between them a long time ago. Now he wondered if he should warn her that he had continued in the same vein with Ben and Kennedy.

But, somehow, fate just didn't seem to want him to.

Hayden came out the front door of the hotel then, closely followed by Alicia and Hudson. Drake and Mai slunk back into the shadows.

"Looks like they got Hudson that super-computer to work with," Drake mused. "I hope to God the chunky twat can rip through some protocols." He cringed when the swear-word came out. For some reason he had always tried to curb his soldiery tendencies when around Mai.

"Hmm. Let us hope so."

Drake watched the trio leave. He wasn't surprised when Alicia Myles turned around and flicked off a quick, two-finger wave. Drake stared after her.

Can't trust a cold-blooded woman.

CHAPTER TWENTY-SIX

The next day was startling - a day of total comedown. Drake, still hyped on the events of the last few days, found himself with no one to chase, no one to follow and no one to kill.

Didn't seem right somehow.

Hudson was ensconced with his new computer inside one of the neighbouring hotels. Hayden and Kinimaka were on constant watch. When asked, Hayden refused to explain how she had acquired such a computer, just that it had come down through 'different channels'. Drake guessed Gates was involved somewhere and asked if the U.S. Secretary of Defence had moved any further forward yet.

"I get the feeling," Hayden said, "that we're on our own down here." She pulled Drake aside and spoke for his ears alone. "And I don't know why, Matt. It feels like we've been left swinging, but then I get a computer when I ask for one through some extremely odd channels. It feels like we're unsupported, but then Gates continues to come through. He sounds like someone's got his balls in a trouser-press - that's what it sounds like."

Drake winced. "Firstly - lay off the ball-crushing metaphors when there's a guy around. Secondly - maybe someone has gotten to him, just like the others in DC. Question is - how?"

"DC's a hive of commerce, sensationalism and corruption," the CIA agent told him. "Without help, we'll never know."

"He's risking a lot then," Drake pointed out. "Helping you."

"What's that supposed to mean?"

"Nothing." Drake gleaned more from the reaction than he wanted to. "How's the Bearded Tit doing?"

Hayden flashed a genuine smile. "Between burger-breaks, beer-breaks, cigarette-breaks and sex sessions with Alicia - not bad."

Drake made a face. "Urrgh."

There was a knock on the door and Mai slipped inside, closely followed by Wells. Alicia uncurled from her position across the room's only sofa. "Can we help you, Jap government?"

Mai turned a sweet smile in her direction. "You may. We would like a progress report."

"Jus' weaving some magic!" Hudson shouted, seemingly stoked up on horse tranquilizers.

Was that how he kept up with Alicia? Drake swatted the cruel thought away and moved to intercept. Mai, however, slipped inside him and met the English SAS woman head on.

Drake blinked. He hadn't even come close to stopping her. Damn, seven years out really did damage the skill-set. He used to be able to live with her, for a few minutes at least. When this Blood King thing was finished, he vowed, he would take a little time to get back into training.

SAS training.

Alicia was getting dangerously close to Mai. "Progress? How about you progress Wells over there and go bang his brains out!"

"How is the Bearded Tit doing?" Mai asked, deadpan.

Alicia stopped and gawked. Drake winced. Damn, he wished he hadn't coined poor old Hudson's nickname, and then spoken it aloud hundreds of times.

Alicia pulled herself together and struck Mai across the face with a resounding slap. Drake stared. Oh my-

Mai still smiled. "When you do make your move," she whispered. "Hit me like a man."

The only thing moving or breathing was Tim Hudson, still the only one oblivious to what was going down. His fingers flew across the keyboard. He laughed when complicated firewalls yielded easily to the power of the CIA computer and his own deft touch. He swigged beer whilst he waited for algorithms to integrate and passwords to crumble.

Alicia stared at Mai for what seemed a lifetime before turning away. Drake knew then how very deeply she cared for Hudson. Old Alicia would have jumped in with both feet. New Alicia was a different prospect.

Hudson blew a raspberry in frustration. "We're into application-layer firewalls now, dudes. Shit that thinks. You see? These deep-packet inspection applications may think they're good, but they play right into my hands," he massaged his fingers excitedly. "If they can steal information first and then eavesdrop then I can do the same-" he paused. "So long as they don't detect me."

Hudson stood up and spun around. "Latest algorithm's gonna take a while."

They drifted out, leaving Hudson and Alicia to 'kill some time'. Wells made sure he remained as close to Mai as humanly possible.

"So," Drake said to him, "you happy with all the Mai-time you're getting?"

Wells looked a little horror-stricken. "You said that out loud, Drake. Fuck!"

Mano Kinimaka positioned himself by the door. Hayden looked back and gave him a wave. "Don't bother. Those two ain't going anywhere."

Drake nodded. "You get that impression too, huh?"

Wells added: "No way would the Alicia I knew and trained back down from a fight. Not a chance in hell."

"Then she would now be dead," Mai said. "Or dying. Perhaps you could have saved her, Mr Wells?"

"I don't like to brag-"

"An old commander would want to save her, would he not? Jump in the line of fire, as they say."

"Myles is a psycho," Wells blurted. "A murderer. She killed her last boyfriend in cold blood just cos he caught her cheating on him. Guy called Milo."

"Well," Mai shrugged, "none of us are perfect."

Kinimaka rumbled up behind them. "So now what? We wait for the amorous twosome to finish and then come back?"

"Amorous?" Hayden laughed, a welcome change of expression to her face of late. "Says the passionate loverrr." She said the last two words in a mock Italian accent.

"It's what my name means," Kinimaka began to explain, and then realised his boss was beating his balls. "And I'll say no more."

Mai looked like she was taking it all in. Drake glanced at his watch. "Anyone hungry? It's after one."

"Nothing else to do," Kinimaka said, shaking his head. "Anyone would think this was already over."

"If that were the case," Hayden told him, "you'd be taking an extended leave in Oahu, my friend.

North shore, I promise you that."

Over? Drake was thinking. No. Not by a long shot.

CHAPTER TWENTY-SEVEN

The Blood King swopped restlessly between three Sat-phones. On the first was his lackey, Ed Boudreau. On the second was his overseer of the ranch back home, a man who went just by the name Claude. On the third was Senator John R. Lender.

The Blood King so loved to make a man break down.

"Please," Lender was begging. "Please. I couldn't go on . . ."

The Blood King grinned. "Beg, you Yankee bastard," his voice was low and guttural, the kind of noise that had sent shards of fear through men since the caveman days.

It was the Blood King's natural voice.

"I do beg. I beg you."

The Blood King left him pleading and addressed Boudreau. "Explain to me, Mr Boudreau, how you lost the controller. Leave nothing out."

Boudreau was succinct, one could give him that. He was dangerous too, but only up to a certain level. The game being played was known in its entirety only to the Blood King, and went far beyond Blackbeard and his two devices. It went deep into Diamond Head itself, and to the very Gates of Hell.

But that was for the future. The Blood King had prepared well. Claude, his ranch supervisor, was attending to the future side of things.

He addressed Claude whilst the other two babbled: "Are our guests uncomfortable?"

"As requested, sir."

"It may be some time, yet, but I will make my way there. Have everything in order. Do not fail me. I believe there are still three on your . . . list?"

"Yes, sir. Preparations are under way."

The Blood King ended the call. It was time to turn his attention back to Boudreau. "Ed," he growled. "Ed," like the sound of a lion crunching bones.

"Sir?" The trepidation in that one word was enough to put the Blood King in a better mood.

"Truth is, Mr Boudreau, I also thought Alicia Myles was an asset. So we are both fools. But we will learn from that?"

"Yes." The flood of relief was obvious.

"Now. Did my techs give you the coordinates of the computer hacker?"

"Yes. I suspect they have an amateur working for them."

"In fact, this person is good. World class, I am told, even to get as far as he has. But my people are better."

"Of course."

"Get to those coordinates, Mr Boudreau, with overwhelming force. And get me the controller. Is that clear?"

"Yes, sir."

The Blood King severed the connection. The naked prisoner trussed up at his feet stared up at him with wet, desperate eyes.

"Did you lure them with the blood trail?" the Blood King asked his men.

"Several sharks are now following us, sir."

"Excellent." The Blood King bent down and drew a knife across the prisoner's wrists and thighs. He took a moment to watch the life-blood begin to pump and then kicked the trussed-up man overboard, taking care to hold the rope that attached him to the ship. "Stop the boat and inflate his life-jacket. The ocean sport is looking good today."

CHAPTER TWENTY-EIGHT

It was late in the afternoon when Hayden called Drake's mobile. The ex-soldier glanced at Kennedy before he answered.

"This must be important."

Kennedy nodded and looked away. Truth be told, her mind was elsewhere. Her boss, Captain Lipkind, had called about thirty minutes back. The questions he asked were questions she had been avoiding for a while now.

How are you really feeling? Have the nightmares subsided? When are you coming back?

And Drake's reply when she finally mentioned her misgivings? Then we need to get some things out in the open. There are some things you don't know . . . that you really need to know.

What the-?

That was when Hayden called. Drake was agreeing to drop everything and head right over. Of course he was.

"Be right behind you." She waved him on ahead, taking a moment for herself and a moment for all those who had died at the hands of Thomas Kaleb. She would never forget them. Not for one day. She still had a purpose to fulfil, somewhere.

She just didn't know here yet.

*****

Drake didn't want to push Kennedy too hard, so he high-tailed it over to the other hotel. The room was full, with only Kinimaka standing watch. Drake pushed to the front.

"What's the score, guys?"

Hayden was almost grinning. "Listen."

Hudson was leaning back and cracking his fingers one by one. "That last one was a hard bastard to crack. Feels like I took the skin off my fingers. Anyhow, in this age of digital information and electronic eavesdropping nothing is secret. Nothing. The trick is to know where to look. I started by writing a simple program that collects information. A gatherer, if you will. I sent it trickling through the-"

"Ok, dude," Hayden rounded on him. "Just tell us what you've got."

"It starts a long time ago. A figure called the Blood King first rose in Russia in the late '80s. There's nothing but snippets, and most of those appear to have been erased."

"Erased?" Hayden repeated. "How? And by whom?"

"I have no idea. But to get rid of that much information must have taken someone a very long time. Or a lot of people a long time. Or-"

"So he has a team of techs erasing his very existence," Hayden nodded. "Makes sense."

"But no one can erase everything. Traces will always remain. Tiny titbits will always be missed. It's just common sense, you know?"

"I get it techno-boy. Get on with it."

"Well, blah, blah, a figure called the Blood King definitely existed in Russia around the late 80s, early 90s. It took me eight hours to confirm just that. But when you get a starting point, that's when you can start digging in earnest. By piecing together various obscure articles I think the man got mega-rich and decided to vanish."

"Mega-rich?" Drake said. "Through crime?"

Hudson smiled at the computer screen and gave it a loving pat. "Ever hear of Southern Cross Vodka?"

Drake blinked and Ben said, "Well, yeah, it's everywhere."

"The Blood King owns Southern Cross." Hudson looked pleased.

"So you're saying our man's a Russian vodka millionaire."

"Not quite."

Hayden almost reached for her gun. "Then what?"

"He also owns Stryanka. And Russian Best. And Vlodsko. Get the idea?"

"Explain it to me."

"The Blood King is actually a vodka king. Officially, a man called Dmitry Kovalenko owns Southern Cross Vodka, but this man, Kovalenko, appears to be the undisputed number one on every single ownership agreement I come across."

"So our Russian millionaire is-"

"Actually a Russian multi-billionaire. A literal king of his country. I got one passage of juicy information. Just one, mind, in two days of searching. Dmitry Kovalenko lives at sea."

"Like-" Ben struggled to speak. "Like a pirate?"

"Just like a pirate. Like Blackbeard, I suppose. His ship is his castle and yet there is no record of it ever being built. He owns and runs a huge empire from his ship, a floating office and home, always moving."

Drake whistled. "And puts figureheads in place to run his companies which he controls like puppets."

"Did you get anything else?" Hayden asked. "Not complaining, but-"

"Just a crumb. The word Stormbringer. More recent, a few years ago actually. It came up through an American back-channel, was even reported to the CIA, but nothing ever came of it."

"So why is it even linked to Kovalenko?"

"His Southern Cross vodka company copyrighted it as the title of their signature bottle. And I mean signature. It sold for 1.4 million per bottle."

There was a dumbstruck silence. Drake contemplated the arrogance and ignorance of the people out there willing to pay such a sum for a bottle of vodka. "Interesting, if appalling, fact," he said. "But so what?"

"In the blurb they wrote that the owner of their company held the name 'dear to his heart'. That phrase, coming from Russians, well maybe it's nothing. Just thought you should know."

"Couldn't that be the name of the artefact?" Ben said. "A very similar name was mentioned by Calico Jack's scribe."

"This is real news," Hayden looked like she wanted to lean in and kiss Hudson. Alicia quickly perched herself on his knee. In another few seconds she had already started to wriggle suggestively.

Outside the windows, darkness was starting to fall.

Hayden hadn't looked happier since Drake last saw her on a night out in York shooting chocolate vodkas in the Slug.

"Let's leave the lovebirds alone," the CIA agent said. "And go make some calls."

CHAPTER TWNETY-NINE

Alicia Myles squirmed a little more before turning around to face Hudson. "Damn, Huddo, you're good."

With a practised movement she manoeuvred both legs so that she straddled him and began to grind her bottom into his crotch.

"I know that. Is there something else you want?"

"I don't ask, Hudson. You should know that by now."

Alicia nodded towards the bed. Hudson grabbed her by the waist and carried her over before falling unceremoniously among the covers, tangling them in a heap. Alicia laughed and fought her way on top.

"You did a good job today, lover."

"It's why you keep me around."

"Well . . . you have other uses too." Alicia pulled her tight T-shirt off over her head and flung it into the air. Hudson's eyes glazed a little as she reached beneath herself and started to unbuckle his trousers. Within minutes they were both naked, sweat slicking their bodies. Alicia rode him wildly, letting the moment take her away.

It was in these moments that she felt free. Only in these moments.

When Hudson started to strain too much or got a bit too carried away she plucked another short hair from his beard to keep him in the game. Useful things - beards.

189

The nightmares she lived with, day to day, began to fade as the pleasure took hold. The release she craved from the things she'd done grew a little less important. With Hudson, maybe she had found someone with which to make a fresh start. Maybe.

With a fluid movement she flipped herself over and scrambled onto all fours. Hudson took up position behind her, his eyes ablaze with lust as they ran over her naked, waiting body.

"Get stuck in, Huddo," she breathed. "Stop tossing it off."

He thrust forward, making her gasp. She threw her head back, hair whipping her own spine. The feeling of pleasure and lust inside began to mount. There was the urge, the overwhelming feeling, the bliss and nothing else. At last.

Freedom.

The noise of the hotel-room door being barged in cut right through her cravings. It was harsh, sudden, shocking.

Then, as she twisted her body around, Hudson's head exploded above her, showering her and the bed and the windows with blood and other matter. Her lover's headless body slumped beside her before the sound of the gunshot entirely died away.

With his heat still inside her.

Alicia leapt off the bed to face her attackers. Three men stood there, guns in hand, pausing to stop and smirk now as they saw the fully naked woman defenceless before them.

"Look all you want," Alicia Myles hissed. "It's the last eyeful any of you will ever get."

She bounded at the nearest, springing like a cat, and slamming her hard body into his chest. The man staggered back into the wall but kept hold of his weapon. Alicia was on her knees. Within seconds her stiffened palm slammed into his testicles, crushing them, making him double over and making him scream. Alicia spun across the floor, using her bare knees to pivot and gain speed, and crashed into the legs of the second man just as he fired his semi-automatic. Bullets stitched across the hotel-room's ceiling, digging gouges out of the plaster and spraying dust everywhere.

Alicia wrenched the gun from his hand.

"Stare at this shitsack!" Spinning the weapon she fired before her adversary could even gasp. He shot backwards, dead already. From her kneeling position Alicia sent quick eyes at the third man. He was focused on her, gun raised, squeezing the trigger, a hair's-breadth from firing . . . her shot destroyed his knees a millisecond before he fired. The man slammed to the floor in a bloody tangle, his bullet zinging harmlessly into the carpet.

Alicia turned, glimpsing the man she had de-balled desperately trying to bring his weapon around.

Sensing victory she stood up, unashamed. With a slow, deadly deliberation she glided to his side and twisted his wrist so that his own gun barrel stared him in the eyes.

"Eyes that have seen too much," she whispered. "Need putting out."

She squeezed the trigger and turned away. That left one man, the one with the mangled knees. "Who sent you?" she tried. "Was it the Blood King? Did he find us?" She squatted beside him. "Tell me, arsehole. Or I'll start with your bollocks, and work my way up. You know I can do it."

He knew alright. His eyes showed that he was aware of her reputation. And yet still all three of them had hesitated when they saw her naked. Behold the simplicity of men.

She dared not glance at the bed. Dared not think about her lover. The harsh reality might tear her to pieces.

"Boudreau. It was Boudreau. He sent us."

"For me?" Alicia pressed.

"For all of you."

The words sent a black wave crashing through her. For all of you. She smashed the man's face until it bled. "How many? How many has that maniac sent?"

"So many . . . so many . . ." the words were punctuated with agonised gasps. "I couldn't count."

CHAPTER THIRTY

Without looking back, Alicia Myles flung on trousers and a T-shirt and sprinted away from the only man she had ever contemplated a future with. The mellowness that had started to eat away at her bitter edges, the laughter that had started to soothe her soul, disintegrated like so much confetti in the rain, leaving nothing but the razor-edge mind of a stone-cold killer.

Mobile crammed against her forehead she ran like a maniac, gun waving, still coated in blood, and all who saw her shied away and started reaching for cell-phones of their own.

"Drake? Pineapple! We're done. Hudson's . . . dead," the words tangled in her throat. "There's a bloody army on its way. You hear me, fuckhead?"

*****

Drake heard a hundred emotions in Alicia's frantic tones. Chief among them was distress. And it was over the death of Tim Hudson. He felt a moment's sorrow before the code-word pineapple! really struck home.

"Cover the lobby. We'll be there in three minutes."

Hayden was already frowning at him. The others were engaged in conversation.

"We're compromised. The Blood King has found us."

His words struck the room dead. "Don't worry," he spoke to them all. "We'll get through this."

"Leave it all!" Hayden shouted, already on the move. "We only need the controller."

Kinimaka was at her side. Drake motioned Ben and Kennedy to follow and brought up the rear with Wells and Mai. As a group, they flew out of the room and down the corridor towards the stairs. The good thing was he heard no sound of fire coming from below. Perhaps the main force hadn't arrived yet.

Which would allow them to fade away, slip down a few back alleys, steal a mini-van maybe, head for Fort Lauderdale.

They pounded down the stairs. Hayden banged through the door that led to the lobby and swung her CIA issue into a two-handed pose as she moved forward. Kinimaka fanned out to her right, brushing by the enormous fish tank. Drake pushed past Ben and Kennedy, eyes sweeping the three front entrances and trying to penetrate the darkened grounds outside.

Alicia hovered near the big desk. A different pretty girl stood behind it now, her face betraying how concerned she was about Alicia's appearance.

Drake moved towards the girl. "Leave," he nodded towards the back. "Please. Now."

He'd seen the furtive movement outside. But his warning came too late for them all. The hotel's front windows shattered as multiple weapons opened fire.

Tons of shards and sheets of glass came crashing down in a deadly avalanche. Everyone dived for cover as bullets pinged and whizzed around the lobby, thudding into plaster walls and concrete beams and earthenware pots.

Drake dived on top of Ben and immediately began to shuffle them both across the plush carpet towards the hotel's check-in desk, using sheer brute force.

"If only my mum could see me now," Ben grunted, but at least he was keeping his chin up.

Drake grabbed him in a bear hug and double-rolled them behind the heavy desk. A few feet in front of him the desk clerk was on her knees, screaming. Blood soaked a patch on her shoulder.

Drake scooted across. "Listen to me," he shouted. "Listen! Doing nothing will get you killed. Now, go."

He manhandled her towards the door that led to the back office. Not safe by any means, but safer than where she had been. A figure came around the corner of the desk, Kennedy, which made Drake exhale a gulp of relief. One of these damn days he was going to have to start carrying a gun.

But then, it was so much cheaper prying them from the hands of his dead enemies.

The sound of running boots galvanised Drake further. These bastards were taking no prisoners, attacking with devastating force and only one goal in mind. The ex-soldier popped up his head quickly to take in the scene.

Ruined front windows. His heart skipped several beats to see a group of tourists huddled over by the potted plants in the corner. They weren't taking cover, just sitting there in shock, and the Blood King's men were taking a bead on them.

"No!"

It did no good except to draw unwanted attention. Madness prevailed, as it had through every step of this Caribbean nightmare, as the innocents were shot dead. Now Drake could hear a voice screaming above all the noise, a voice that could only belong to Ed Boudreau.

From somewhere, Hayden and Kinimaka were firing back. The first wave of killers were quickly decimated as they ran into the hotel and collapsed, blocking the path of those running behind them.

Drake used the disruption to vault the check-in desk. He landed and rolled to the left, scooping up a weapon as he went. In another moment he was smack-bang in the middle of a melee. The enemy came at him from all sides, too close to use weapons effectively, but striking with arms and heads and knees. Drake blocked and ducked and side-stepped, but still he would have faltered if it wasn't for Hayden and Kinimaka clinically taking out every man around him. Then, as if Christmas had come early, Mai had waded in to his right and Alicia was to his left. Killing machines both, they cut a swath of destruction through the bad guys. Mai ended a life with every strike of her limbs. Alicia hurt or maimed a man with every punch. Drake used the gun.

For a moment the enemy onslaught faltered.

Then Drake saw the second wave coming, armed to the teeth, and he knew this night was far from over.

"Cover!" he cried. "Regroup to cover. Now!"

CHAPTER THIRTY-ONE

Using the carnage as cover, Drake and his comrades made for the back stairs. Drake remembered to drag the terrified clerk with them, putting Ben in charge of her.

"Babysitting duty," he muttered. "Bit of a U-turn for ya."

Their rooms had been prepped. The bad guys couldn't know where the controller was being kept so would have to exercise some caution, at least. They left Kinimaka watching the stairs. When they dog-legged past the corridor that led to the small bank of lifts Wells stopped them by saying: "Any way we can dismantle those?"

Hayden floundered. Mai took immediate control of the suggestion. "You go on. I can take a look."

"I'll back you up." Wells patted his pocket. Drake hoped to God there was a gun in there. He motioned that Alicia take position behind Mai and Wells just in case they needed back-up.

Hayden reached their rooms. It took a moment to make a call. "Alert's out. Cops are already on their way. Army soon after."

"Army?" Drake frowned.

"Figure of speech. SWAT. Marines. Delta, whatever. They're sending whoever's nearest."

"Not convinced the cops are a good idea," Drake said. "They're have no training in-"

Kennedy cut him off. "Cops are better than you give 'em credit for, Matt. Don't spin that inter-agency superiority crap. I've heard a lifetime of it."

"I was just trying to protect them." Drake saw it was no use. "Fine. Ok. I doubt we could stop them anyway."

He ducked back out of the room, leaving Hayden to get on with it. At the far end of the corridor Mai and Wells had called the lift and were staring at something. Alicia was watching, her face a mask of stone. He heard nothing from Kinimaka, so had to assume the stairways were quiet.

He walked down quickly to Alicia. "I didn't realise," he said in a low voice. "About Hudson and you. I just wanted to say I'm sorry. I never knew how much you cared for him."

"He kept them at bay," Alicia said with a faraway look on her face. "You know what I'm talking about Drake. You know."

"That I do. But you can find happiness, Alicia. You know that now."

Alicia's face turned stormy. "Don't patronise me, Drakey. No way have you found eternal happiness with that fucked-up cop. Not a chance in hell."

"I didn't mean-" Ah, what was the point? he thought. Everyone was always misunderstanding him.

Mai and her shadow, Wells, came trotting back. "I ripped out the control mechanism," Mai reported.

"Should slow them down a little, if they were ever dumb enough to consider using the lift in the first place."

"They were," Drake said. "And not because they're dumb but because the man driving them is insane."

"Boudreau's beyond certifiable," Alicia said. "He'd send a hundred men over the barricades just to check if it was raining on that side."

"I meant the Blood King," Drake said. "But I guess they're both crazy."

Kinimaka popped his head around the corner. "Incoming," he breathed as quietly as he could and then started blasting away with his weapon.

Drake smiled. "Levity even in a fire-fight," he said. "Nothing like it."

He raced across to back up the big Hawaiian. There were men flooding the stairwells, trying to gain a foothold by sheer force of numbers. Kinimaka would run out of ammo before he stopped them all.

Doors were cracking open up and down the corridors. Drake roared at them all to get inside and stay there until the cops arrived. Most complied. Those few that didn't might well be on their own.

"Fall back," Drake signalled Mai and Alicia to cover them as they flew up the corridor. "We'll man this corner too. Make every step as costly for them as possible."

Mai smiled sweetly. "That's what we do."

Drake raced on, dragging the Hawaiian with him. Hayden was stood half-way out the door. "Progress?"

"Cops are imminent. I can hear the sirens. We need to see what goes down."

Drake indicated the other two rooms they had purchased. "They overlook the front and left-hand sides."

Hayden took off, motioning that Kinimaka should keep watch. They unlocked the furthest room and moved cautiously towards the windows. Even from half-way Drake could see the flashing lights. They seemed to fill up half the roads in Miami.

"My God," he breathed.

Hayden sucked in a breath. "There's no way this can end well. No way at all. Drake, we need to get this controller out of here. Now."

Drake was thinking hard. "How many civilians do you reckon are staying here, Hayden?"

"Drake!"

"What?"

"Do you want a madman calling the shots? Plundering the economy? Setting impossible goals?"

"Would we notice the difference?" Drake couldn't resist. "Sorry, just kidding. I know, I know. No time for it. I can't leave these people to face that madman's army, Hayden, so make your own choice. Look, I know I'm not your boss, but it could be more dangerous out there than if you stay here. For you and the controller."

Hayden's face revealed her uncertainty. For once, the CIA agent seemed at a loss.

"There are some major players here," Drake pushed a little. "Mai's the best. Wells, he's ok and could bring an army of his own in about thirty minutes. And Alicia, she's pretty formidable when she's on our side."

"That depends on what colour pants she's wearing, if any." Hayden flashed a weak smile.

"We do have the high ground," Drake assured her as they exited the room. "Technically speaking."

Gunfire echoed along the corridor. Something even louder rocked the night around the front of the hotel.

Drake headed back into the room.

It was going to be a long night.

*****

The scene outside the hotel reminded him of war zones he'd visited. Miami P.D. had barricaded the streets as far as he could see. Hundreds and hundreds of black-and-whites and police vans were cordoning off the area. Figures dressed in bullet-proof vests were approaching the 'hot' zone even as Drake watched with a shiver of trepidation running down his spine.

Boudreau would have expected the law.

When the police advanced to within ten metres of the hotel grounds the seemingly impossible happened. Half a dozen car bombs exploded, traps that the cops had walked right past. At the same time shooters hidden in nearby buildings opened fire, picking off cops like plastic ducks at a fairground shooting gallery.

Fire and metal bloomed high into the air, crashing down amidst panicked men.

Drake watched the horror and the slaughter for another minute. If this was the force that Boudreau and the Blood King were willing to bring to bear then that changed his outlook somewhat. Maybe Hayden had been right. Maybe it was time to get out of this death-trap.

Time for Plan B.

He ran out of the room, relaying to Hayden what he'd seen and telling her to mobilise. When he reached the corridor junction he paused. Kinimaka and Alicia were keeping the enemy at bay with sparse covering fire, but when Drake risked a peek around the corner he saw something that made his blood run cold.

Boudreau's men were starting to drag people out of their rooms. They were herding them into a group and were clearly going to force them forward and use them as cover.

Kinimaka stared at Drake with frantic eyes.

This wouldn't stand.

Drake stepped into the open and began to advance. In full sight he breathed deeply, took careful aim, and began squeezing shots off. One shell whizzed through the curls of a blonde-woman's hair to smash through the forehead of the mercenary behind her. The second shell grazed past a man's neck and destroyed the throat of his aggressor. The third found an enemy who popped his own head up in shock.

Drake continued forward, calm, focused. One of the enemy soldiers hit the deck and fired a shot off. The bullet tugged at Drake's jacket but he only needed a millisecond to readjust. His fourth bullet sent the man spinning against the corridor wall, painting the blue wallpaper in crimson whorls.

He reached the group. The hotel guests ducked as he went by. He took a brief moment to fire off more shots until his clip ran empty before herding the shell-shocked people into the nearest room.

He studied them for the one who looked most capable.

"That's all I can do for you. Now you have to help yourselves." He'd addressed a tough dude who looked like a biker and had been sheltering his wife with his own humongous arms. "Barricade the door after me. Make it hard for them to get in here and they won't even bother trying. And find something you could use as a weapon. Anything."

Drake exited the room, confident that both Kinimaka and Alicia would be laying down enough covering fire to facilitate his escape. He left the empty gun with the guests. Last resort kind of thing.

"How's the ammo?" he asked Kinimaka when he reached the junction.

"Low. Maybe half a dozen shots left."

Alicia nodded grimly. "Three."

"We're getting out of here. Conserve what you can."

He entered their room. Ben was sitting with the desk-clerk on the leather sofa, making eyes at her and trying to lighten her fear. It was never going to work, but Drake thought it was a good way to occupy the kid's time. Kennedy, Mai and Wells were staring out of the big windows. This part of the hotel was around the corner from the entrance but they could still see part of the fire-fight going on out there. Flames and bullet traceries and the screams of sirens still tore holes through the night.

Alicia leapt through the door behind him. "I'm out."

"Time to go," Drake told them. "Move."

Ben and the desk-clerk were up and past him quickly, his words music to their ears. The other three started to walk towards him and at that moment there was a terrible noise as if the very fabric of the hotel had shattered.

The room's windows exploded. Fragments of glass burst across the room. Kennedy lost her footing and fell face first across the sofa. Mai and Wells staggered but bounced off each other after a momentary embrace.

In all this bedlam why on earth was Wells smiling?

Got some Mai-time, he mouthed at Drake.

Drake didn't move as glass shards rained around him. Bullets now fizzed and rocketed through the empty window panes. The bad guys below had found their room and were making life even more difficult.

Boudreau's evil voice drifted up. "Come out, come out little pigs!" Then he started to squeal like a pig being slaughtered, his screaming louder than all the bullets and the explosions and even the random gunfire coming from the hallway.

The madness had taken him completely. It had never been far away.

Drake ushered Kennedy out the door, shielded by Kinimaka's bulk, and down the dog-leg towards the far room. He started to follow when there was the shocking sound of close-up gunfire behind him.

Just one shot.

He turned instantly. The scene that greeted him numbed even his jaded battleground emotions. Wells was lying on his side, twitching slightly, a red pool spreading from the side of his head. Both Mai and

Alicia were stood watching him, guns lowered, showing no sign of concern or offering any assistance whatsoever.

Drake stared from one woman's eyes to the other. "What happened?"

Alicia jerked a hand towards the window. "In case you haven't noticed, Drakey, there's bullets flying everywhere. Poor old bastard got clipped."

Drake stared at Wells' motionless body, finding it hard to weigh his feelings for the old man, his Commander, a man of unspeakable secrets.

There wasn't time now.

Mai stared Drake right in the eyes. "The secrets that man kept," she shook her head a little. "I can't say that I mourn his passing."

More bullets shattered through the walls and ceiling of the hotel room.

Drake had no time to consider what had really happened in the room when his back was turned. Chief problem being - if one of the women had killed Wells why were they both keeping quiet about it?

Kinimaka looked relieved when they came running out and immediately abandoned his post. "One round left," he breathed.

As he ran, Drake wondered about that. Alicia had said she was out. That left Mai with the smoking gun. But then, the ex-SAS Englishwoman could hardly be taken at her word could she?

Hayden had prepped the room. The method of egress they had decided days ago was simple enough, if a little time consuming. One of the small bedroom windows exited upon the tiled roof of a generator building. That roof led to a shed that housed the air-conditioning units which, in turn, led nicely to terra-firma. In addition, the whole area was shrouded by palm trees, clearly an effort made by the hotel management to hide the offending utility buildings.

Plan B.

Of course, Drake knew it wasn't perfect; even by David Beckham's standards it was a long shot from a guaranteed escape route.

Alicia and Mai went first, two deadly combatants leading the way. Hayden followed with the controller under her jacket and then came Kinimaka and Kennedy. Drake supervised Ben and the desk-clerk and brought up the rear. By the time he climbed out of the window he had heard no sound of pursuit and allowed himself a brief sigh of relief.

The balmy Miami air struck his skin with a welcome touch. An intense din - the sound of combat - assailed his hearing. Being cynical, the din would help mask their movements. Truly, it was horrifying.

With shoes slipping and squeaking across the hard tile roof the seven escapees made their way to solid ground. The branches of the palm trees around them swayed eerily, their hard, thin, resolute trunks standing watch like soldiers guarding a frontier. Drake trusted Mai and Alicia to sniff them a way out.

It occurred to him then, with quiet revelation, that he didn't have as much belief in anyone else he knew, including Kennedy. More baggage to overcome.

Mai paused at the tree-line. Beyond that Drake could see a dimly lit parking-lot, jam-packed with vehicles but devoid of life.

Mai spun around. Drake read her mind. Risky, but worth it. A typical Plan B.

The Japanese agent went first, skipping lightly over a flagged path into the lot, disappearing between cars. No shouts of alarm went up. Alicia followed next, just as graceful. They both crouched beside a gigantic Dodge Ram and signalled to the others to wait.

Mai edged close to the front of the Dodge and surveyed the area for a second before beckoning the rest over. Drake brought up the rear. To the left, a horde of mercenaries milled and glared up at the hotel room they had blasted apart, the hotel room where Commander Wells of the SAS lay dead. Boudreau was among them somewhere, but Drake could not see him. To the ex-SAS man's right the few mercenaries he saw were concentrating their attentions towards their outskirts, rather than on anyone sneaking about in their midst.

Hunched down against the Ram, Drake took a moment to think. If they could make it to the exit and find a nearby vehicle large enough, they might all be able to high-tail it out of here before the bad guys cottoned on.

"Exit?" he whispered along the line to Mai.

The petite woman nodded and started crab-walking away. In a few minutes they were all threading between the deserted rows with the mayhem receding at their backs. Ben even had time to try and help the desk-lady crab-walk, receiving an unhappy shove in reward.

Time passed. The night deepened. They spied the big exit sign and Drake spotted a big Chevrolet Tahoe a few bays down. "Who's got hot-wiring skills?" he hissed.

At that moment there was a commotion way behind them. From all the shouting it was clear the mercenaries inside the hotel had noticed their escape, if not its route. No doubt they would be communicating straight to Boudreau.

A squeal went up like an animal in pain. Yeah, Boudreau knew.

Alicia was already on her way, smashing the Tahoe's window and climbing inside. Within seconds she had silenced the alarm, but the damage was already done.

The Blood King's men were here.

Vaulting over cars and running between bays, they came at them at pace. Drake, Alicia, Mai, Hayden and Kinimaka stood to face them. The bad guys didn't even have time to bring their weapons to bear. Drake flew at them, stiff-arming a man in the face, grabbing the neck of another and spinning him so viciously his neck snapped. He took an elbow to the side of the head, turned and snarled at the offender who stepped back in surprise. Drake made a show of lunging for the man and smiled nastily when he shrank away.

"You be fucked, little man," Drake hissed and struck out with both hands. The man went down choking, suffocating to death. Drake had a brief moment to realise that that was the old SAS soldier. He was still in there somewhere.

Maybe the presence of Mai had made the old soldier surface. Or was it Alicia? Damn all these women.

Speaking of Mai he watched her work. God, the artistry of it. That woman could turn murder into an art form. Blood ran and bones snapped in her wake. Men stared after her, shocked, confused, holding their guts in their hands. Mai was ruthless. Without her, Drake and the rest would have struggled. With her they won the day in five pitiless minutes.

Only once did she falter. Only once . . . when she fell against Hayden, and Hayden went down. Men landed atop them. Punches flew. Gun barrels were smashed into skulls. Mai took half a second to meet Drake's eyes . . . and received the nod of approval.

Hayden never felt it or saw it coming.

Then, the melee miraculously ended as the tiny Japanese woman came up fighting, adding to her already impressive body count. Even Alicia took a second to watch her.

Then, there was a moment's respite. They all bolted for the Chevy. Alicia took the wheel again and resumed her hot-wiring. The Tahoe's engine caught.

"Drive!"

Eight cylinders propelled the Tahoe at a surprising rate, considering its homely looks. The Chevy shot forward and bounced up the slight ramp, out of the lot and onto a wide, uninhabited street.

From their right came the sounds of gunfire. The cops and 'whoever else' - in Hayden's words - fighting it out with the Blood King's men. More shots soon came from their rear.

The Chevy shuddered as several struck home. When Drake glanced out the window to his left he saw men running across the parking-lot, rifles held in front of them, tracking them all the way.

"Step on it," he urged.

"Nooo!"

Hayden suddenly screamed. "I lost the controller! I lost it!"

Mai lowered her window, aiming the only rifle they had left. She sprayed the lot with covering fire to gain them more time. Three men went sprawling.

Hayden was struggling with the door catch. "No. This is so bad. We can't just leave it."

Drake turned a stony glance in her direction. "Stay put. There are too many of them back there and you know it. We'll come up with something."

"Anyway," Ben said brightly. "They might not find it. Did it just slip out of your jacket?"

"I don't know," Hayden moaned. "One minute it was there . . ."

"Why do they follow this man, this Boudreau?" Mai quickly spoke up. "Even if they survive the battle he gives them up to assist his escape."

"It's the Blood King they're loyal too," Drake said speculating just as fast. "Because he offers them the only thing they care about. Money. I bet each and every one is on a special, lucrative contract."

"A sort of 'return whenever and you'll get paid' contract?" Kennedy shrugged. "That'd do it for most of 'em. Scum of the earth."

"So even if they get caught and put in jail they still get paid when they get out?" Hayden looked dubious. "Well, I guess it's a quick way to build a loyal army."

Several more bullets thunked into the Tahoe.

Kinimaka was staring intently ahead. "Say, isn't that the Bank of America? Always wanted to see it up close."

"Can't you people hear that!" The desk-clerk suddenly screamed, making them all jump higher than if an RPG had just fizzed past. "There's bullets hitting the car. Bullets!"

Drake stared at her as if she was mad. "We didn't think it was kids throwing peanuts, love."

Ben patted her hand. "Don't worry, miss. This is how we roll."

Drake groaned. "Give it a rest, Iggle Piggle. We'll be out of range soon, Miss."

Ben said: "That's right, hit me where - say, where's Wells?"

"You're only just missing him?" Hayden lowered her eyes. "Sorry. He died back there."

Drake saw a look pass between Mai and Alicia. The waters ran deep between them, a deluge of bad memories and secrets he was hoping he wouldn't have to delve into.

The Tahoe was heading towards one of the police cordons. Hayden eyed it with pleasure. "Thank you, god."

"Just remember Jonathan's words," Drake reminded her, ever watchful. "Trust no one. Tell them as little as possible."

The cordon came up quick. Alicia let the car drift to a non-threatening halt.

Nothing moved. The barricade was deserted.

Alicia looked around at Drake and pulled a face. "Fuckin' great." English irony.

Then, a man walked through the barriers, a man walking very fast and with a big metal briefcase bashing his legs.

Hayden sat up in surprise. "That's Justin Harrison." She rolled down the window.

Harrison came up quick and stopped next to the gently ticking Tahoe. He stared at Hayden. "You really need to strip all your clothes off, Miss Jaye, right now."

Drake fancied you could have heard a pin drop.

Harrison blinked. "For your own sake, naturally."

CHAPTER THIRTY-TWO

"We've been tracking you the whole time," Harrison told them as Hayden and Kinimaka exited the car. "You have the controller. I don't think there's a more important person in the world than you now, Miss Jaye."

Hayden thought about the trackers they'd implanted in her clothing. "Shit, there's even one in my pants." She half-laughed. "Hope you've brought your credit card, Harrison."

Drake leaned out the window. "Is it a case of trusting no one? Or just being careful?"

"Both," said Harrison shrugging. "Clearly, I can't say much. I don't know much."

"Trust a politician." Drake laughed and then draped himself out the window. "So, you gonna start stripping then?"

Kennedy slapped him. Kinimaka looked a little affronted. "I didn't mean you, big boy."

"Seriously," Harrison came around the front as Kinimaka and Hayden climbed back in, "that's an imperative. If there is a mole on the surveillance side we can't have them relaying our whereabouts to Boudreau."

"Ok, ok, I'll strip," Hayden said. "Just get me some damn clothes first. Or at least a blanket."

Ben couldn't hide a grin. "Wish I'd have come up with that ploy."

But Hayden was leaning close to Harrison now, no doubt imparting the bombshell that she actually didn't have the controller any more. That it was lost back at the parking lot. Harrison's head went down immediately.

Alicia started the car and drove carefully through the barricade. Military personnel melted back into sight now that Harrison had done his thing, hard-faced men with steel in their eyes.

Kennedy was rummaging around in the boot. "There's a blanket back here and a trench-coat. That ok for you?"

With some difficulty and averting of eyes and intense shuffling both Hayden and Kinimaka stripped totally naked and threw their clothes out the window. Alicia Myles was, perhaps predictably, the only one of the bunch who watched the entire proceedings, examining Mano with enthusiastic interest. In a way, Drake didn't mind so much. At least it showed the real Alicia was still present.

Hayden donned the trench-coat. Kinimaka wrapped his bulk inside the blanket. Everyone pretended not to notice the flesh that remained uncovered.

Hayden leaned forward with extreme caution. "Harrison. Do you guys have a plan? What's been going on?"

The Secretary of Defence's aide smiled genuinely for the first time since Drake had known him. "Ah, yes. Do we have a plan."

*****

Harrison directed Alicia to head back towards the Keys for now. "Just keep driving, Miss Myles, we have a facility on the way."

Alicia looked at him. "Did Hudson's information help you?"

"Tip o' the sword, Miss Myles, tip o' the sword. It was the edge we needed to carve our way into Dmitry Kovalenko's shady world. And by shady I mean black. In every way. The legend says that the Blood King kills a man every single day, just because he can. If his crew don't fetch him a worthwhile prisoner, he kills one of the crew."

"Where did all this new information come from?" Drake asked cautiously.

"Using Hudson's information as a starting point we back-tracked through history. Came up with some interesting links to people within our reach, if you know what I mean. In short, the Blood King has helped some pretty powerful people become powerful over the last twenty years. All we had to do was start squeezing those people and piece together the information."

"Squeezing them?" the desk-clerk asked with a tremor in her throat.

Harrison did a double-take. "Where did she come from?"

"The front desk," she moaned.

Harrison stared around silently.

"We can't just ditch her," Drake said. "Carry on. She'll be fine, won't you love?"

The desk-clerk looked away, straight at Kinimaka, then blushed and stared at the floor.

"Kovalenko rose to power when Russia was at its weakest, sometime after the cold war. His family owned a vodka refinement plant, which he quickly turned into a world class brand by forcing the best people to work for him. Kind of like what he's doing now, though we still don't know how."

"Or who." Drake's barb was like a left hook.

"Indeed. Kovalenko then set about acquiring most of the other vodka brands in Russia, in secret. He wanted to be the undisclosed owner rather than partner, the man behind it all, but never seen. His empire, well it is almost unlimited. We've just scratched the surface and found over three hundred companies he owns."

"So why did he chose to do a Blackbeard?" Ben asked. "You know, live at sea like a pirate?"

"It's what gave him his anonymity. You know, someone says 'he lives at sea' and wonders why he can't be found. What most people don't understand is that the seas are unbelievably vast. There are many, many thousands of square miles of ocean that, though charted, are never sailed or tracked. The manpower required to do so would be nonsensical."

Harrison had been talking fast-like-a-fox now for some time. Drake saw no sign of him taking a break. Hayden asked him about Boudreau.

"Far as we know, he's just a merc. The Blood King, with his resources, could have recruited anybody. Maybe Boudreau came recommended."

"Only by Top Psycho Magazine," Kennedy shivered despite the heat in the car.

"So, Kovalenko sailed these waters for twenty years," Drake pointed out. "And was never seen? Come on, Justin. Pull the other one."

"No thank you. The Blood King was seen, Drake. Of course he was seen. The ship he had commissioned, though we haven't located it yet, we're guessing is beyond cutting edge. But it won't look more than a spit different to any other hundred-million-dollar yacht out there. And, trust me, there's more than you would think."

"He'd send crew ashore for provisions," Ben said. "Using the ship's tenders. Why, though, would the crew want to spend their lives at sea with him?"

"The pirates did it," Harrison said. "The Blood King is just a modern day version. Maybe he pressed them all into service. A lifetime of indenture to provide their families with riches, or save them from bandits or whatever. You gotta see that when you have the Blood King's power and resources, nothing is impossible."

Kinimaka made a backwards motion. "Like starting a war in Miami?"

"Just like that."

Alicia threaded the Tahoe through some traffic onto a much wider road. "Do I get my pardon, Mr Government Stooge?"

219

To his credit, Harrison didn't even look at her. "Let's revisit that subject later, hmm? But I will tell you one other thing."

"Whenever you're ready."

"That name Hudson uncovered - Stormbringer? It's not only the name of the device . . . it's also the name of the Blood King's ship."

"'Dear to our owners heart.'" Alicia remembered the snippet her dead lover had found. "Of course it was. Since he commissioned it and lived on it."

"We will find the ship," Harrison said. "Our only concern is how much warning he will have that we are coming."

"Send in the biggest damn thing that you've got," Drake told him. "The bastard likes big odds. Send him bigger odds than even he can handle."

Harrison smiled. "Every carrier and warship we have around the world is on standby."

CHAPTER THIRTY-THREE

"Do you think the Blood King knew of the device?" Ben asked as the darkness began to soften outside the car's windows. "And named his ship after it?"

"Sure. The coincidence otherwise just doesn't wash."

"Then why didn't he fetch it himself?"

"Well, this leads us in to the next phase of his plan," Harrison paused. "We think."

"Next phase?" Drake came alert.

"Kovalenko never knew where the displacement device ended up. He could not have known it sank aboard the Queen Anne's Revenge or, as Ben says, he wouldn't have hesitated to obtain it. They've been digging that old wreck up for a decade."

"So the TV coverage was most likely his biggest shock since he came firing down the birth canal?" Drake wondered.

Hayden nodded. "And then he sent a team to grab the CIA agents in charge of investigating the case. Full circle."

"We beat him to the controller," Ben pointed out. "That's why he sent Alicia to grab us in Key West."

"But you said something about a next phase," Kinimaka said.

"This isn't the Blood King's big play," Harrison said. "It's something that has diverted him momentarily from his plan. I mean, think of the sheer fortune of seeing the device, the chance that it would be shown on TV, and then the gut reaction. It all smacks of a man seeking his dream rather than his goal."

"Is that all you got?" Drake screwed up his face.

"No. A good third of the people we, um, spoke to, told us the Blood King had been searching for something extremely precious for his entire life. Something even he, with all his power, couldn't get his hands on. They also said he was nearing the end of his quest. He has properties all over the world in addition to his floating home you know, and it is one of these that he plans to retire to soon and so fulfil a lifelong quest."

"Still ball-all to go on," Drake snapped. "Do you have locations?"

"Some. Every time Kovalenko elaborated on this quest, he would simply refer to it as 'reaching for the gates of hell'. He also apparently banged on about Cook finding it first. That bastard Cook found it first, to quote one source."

"Captain Cook?" Kinimaka sounded surprised. "The man who came to Hawaii?"

"Most likely. We don't know."

"That all means nothing," said Mai who had been so quiet up until then that Drake had almost forgotten she was there. Calm, but taking everything on board. "And if we destroy him now?"

"I so admire the plain thinking of the Japanese," Harrison said. "Our thoughts too. Once we have him in custody - or dead - his plans evaporate with him."

Kennedy was squirming about on the leather seat, still trying to pull those jeans up a little more. "You can bet your ass on one thing. In addition to an army, he'll have some radical defences on that ship."

Hayden gave the New York cop a sassy look. "I'll take those jeans off your hands if you like, Ken. You got no idea what bits I'm getting stuck to the leather."

Kinimaka shifted a bit. "I do."

"Hey, talky dude," Alicia barked. "How much friggin' further do you want me to go? Normally, people pay to keep me in one position for so long."

"Key Largo," Harrison stared at a passing signpost. "We have a facility there. A most interesting one. Won't be long now."

"Will it help you find the Blood King's ship?" Drake asked.

Harrison smiled but the emotion didn't touch his eyes. "With this masterwork of technology, Mr Drake, you could see through the walls of . . . " he gulped a little. "Well, you'll see. It's good."

*****

Key Largo might well have been the largest of the Keys' archipelago but within twenty minutes Alicia was unhappily waving the famous Caribbean Club goodbye and pulling into a concealed entrance. Within seconds a small, squat building appeared. Harrison directed Alicia to pull up outside and indicated a masked entryway to the side.

"Let's go."

Around the side of the building they entered the main complex. Harrison showed his credentials and immediately ordered new clothes for Hayden and Kinimaka. The facility administrator eyed the big man dubiously.

"We may have to send out for you, sir."

Kinimama nodded, used to it. "Whatever, man, whatever you can do."

"And this woman," Harrison indicated the desk-clerk. "Needs to be debriefed."

Harrison led them towards the inner workings of the facility. Drake walked behind Kennedy, aware that the two white elephants who shared their room had only gotten bigger during the last few days. He felt driven to help Hayden, to enable her to come to terms with the loss of her men, but at the same time he knew Kennedy and he hadn't fared well recently.

Was it some kind of comedown for her? Not being able to quietly keep in contact with some of the relatives. Or was she continuing it by mobile, through Twitter maybe. In any case she remained distant and uncommunicative, which made him worry further.

Life had been so much simpler in the SAS. Listen, obey, execute. Just do your job.

Real life made everything turn to grey. It slowed him down and sucked away his fighting and thinking prowess. This was because real life wasn't as straightforward and simple as living the army life.

It was because real life was the toughest boot camp in the world.

And now it tore at him that when he needed his army skills the most he had sat on his arse, diluting them for over seven years.

The main room in the facility was round, and circuited above by a walkway that provided access to banks of flashing terminals that lined the walls. Three operatives stood around chatting until they saw Harrison speed-walking towards them.

"Sir?"

"I need a briefing of where we're at and how we got there. Now."

The facility's team leader came forward, proffering a hand and then pointing out a row of hi-tech terminals that sat below a bank of TV screens mounted on the wall.

"A demonstration is usually quicker," he said. "Then the explanation."

The tech sat down without inviting anyone to join him and started pecking at a few buttons. Within seconds a grainy image started to emerge on the screens.

"Just tasking our baby," he muttered to himself. "There she is, there . . ." he finessed a pair of toggles as he pecked away. "It's normally quicker, but we put her on stand-by. Poor girl's had a rough few days."

Kennedy grunted at him. "Some of us have had a rough few years."

Drake laid a hand on her shoulder. At least she didn't shrug it off. When she turned her head slightly he beckoned her over to a quiet corner.

"When this is over," he said, "do you think we could talk? About Kaleb. About the families' victims. And about Alyson?"

It was the first time he'd openly invited talk about his late wife since her death.

Kennedy looked shocked. "You want to? Really?"

"Yes."

"I would," Kennedy nodded immediately. "That would be good."

A series of long beeps interrupted their moment. Drake looked over to see the tech indicating the high screens and a rapidly emerging image. "Ok," he spoke like a college lecturer, "what we have here is your standard satellite image, as seen . . . " he bowed his head," . . . on many a TV show. This is what you, the general public, are used to."

Drake wondered if he'd really lost it that much. Damn, he needed to get back into that tough regimental training that the Hereford boys did every day.

The classified system zoomed in closer as the tech squeezed a toggle. Within seconds they were looking down at a busy street, so close they could pick out the features of passers-by.

"Paris." The tech told them. "It's around eight a.m. there now. See there? The Park Lane hotel, right in the heart of the Champs-Elysees." The camera whizzed up to the roof, so close Drake could actually see individual pebbles and bits of litter.

"Fantastic," Ben breathed.

"Old hat," the team leader said. With that he squeezed a little harder and the camera panned forward, zipping through the very fabric of the walls.

"Woah," Kennedy said. "I didn't know you could do that."

Now the view showed one of the hotel corridors.

"This?" the tech grinned, "this has been around for a while. You can get this kind of technology on a cell-phone right now. They're marketing it as 'see-through-walls' technology, but they've dumbed it down so you only get to see about four inches in. Privacy laws and all that."

"I should think so," Kennedy told him. "Imagine what a stalker or a killer would use that kind of technology for."

"Agreed. But this is what we use it for."

The tech sent the camera whooshing along the corridor, through the lift doors and down the shaft, and then up the next corridor. Quickly, just to show the scope of the science, he darted into a room where a couple were eating on the bed.

"We tap into a previously unused range in the electro-magnetic spectrum. Combining the terahertz waves with CMOS technology we can actually see anywhere. It's an upgrade to the old Thermal Imaging Satellites that only read body heat. You may have seen satellites that showed people looking like blobs of fire, running around? Well, this is the next step. Clearly, it's had to be classified beyond top secret."

"This doesn't even exist?" Kinimaka looked around. "Cool."

Kennedy was shaking her head. "I can't believe you have this. And that you're pleased with yourselves. You never hear of 'invasion of privacy'?"

"Can it, for Christ's sake will you?" Alicia drawled back at her. "Let the little man get to his point. I'm dying of boredom here."

In reply to Kennedy the tech said: "We're the United States Government, Miss. We do pretty much whatever we want." Then he flicked a shy smile towards the English assassin.

"And my point . . ." he flicked another switch that set off a new set of pictures, "is this. We recorded all this yesterday and today."

The pictures suddenly began to whizz by and then, with sickening quickness, came into perfect focus. Drake smiled to see an enormous vessel laid out before them, what could only be described as a super-yacht.

"Is that what I think it is?" He glanced at Harrison.

"The floating home of Dmitry Kovalenko," he said. "The Stormbringer."

Alicia took a step forward. "So Hudson cracked it," she said with a rare authentic smile. "He actually found the Blood King when no one else could."

"Yes, miss Myles," Harrison took a moment to return the smile. "Mr Hudson did us a great service."

"That he was always good for," Alicia waved at the screens. "Carry on."

"Well, it's a super yacht. Five hundred feet long. Five decks above the water and one below. Cinema, helicopter hangar, car port. Submarines onboard. Probably a medical centre. At least five tenders - small boats used for grocery runs." The tech shook his head in disbelief. "Never underestimate the greed of the super-rich."

Drake was listening hard. "You've mentioned three methods of escape already."

"I know. And that's the one's we know of. Even this baby couldn't get down to the last level, the one below water. It's shielded with some kind of heavy sheet material."

"Where is he?" Alicia and Hayden said, almost at the same time. They both had reason to confront the Blood King.

"Several miles south of the Dominican Republic," the tech told them. "That's deep water just off the Bermuda Triangle."

"The Triangle?" Kinimaka blurted. "That crazy SOB"

"Yes, well the Blood King has several properties in the United States. We think he is steadily making his way towards one. Obviously he is unaware we have located him."

Drake pursed his lips. "Don't be a dick. The man owns you. He knows your every move. You're lucky he's at sea or he'd have disappeared already. Perhaps that, in the end, was his only mistake."

Hayden spoke to Harrison. "What's the plan? You've already mobilised, right?"

Harrison grinned. "Can you say Fort Lauderdale?"

The tech chimed in. "I often do at Spring Break," he said, shooting a grin around, received nothing in return and carried on. "Based there, you got half a dozen USS Destroyers. A fleet of F22-A Raptors. And about sixteen USS submarines. That bastard just sailed near the wrong harbour."

"Did you identify his defence capabilities?" Drake asked.

"Firstly-" Harrison sighed, "a vast amount of men, all armed with the latest weaponry, you can bet your ass. I'm sure he'll have a cupboard full of rocket launchers too. Obviously he can't have deck-mounted gun turrets - that would've drawn to much attention through the years. His capabilities have to be hidden. So, we think defence is his strongpoint. Early warning systems. Laser shields. Armour-plating. Booby-traps. The army of willing men."

"Willing?" Kennedy hissed. "No, they're not willing, count on that. The Blood King's way is through coercion not employment."

Harrison continued with barely a flicker. "Ed Boudreau may also be on board. He has vanished since the last attack."

"All these defences, of course," Drake said, "are designed for just one thing. To give Kovalenko time to escape whilst those who protect him die."

Harrison shrugged. "A plot he has no doubt hatched and re-hatched many times since he became a self-made myth."

"I so wish we could find out what it is he has over all these people," Ben said.

Harrison pursed his lips. "Well, it has to be something big. He sure owns some connected people."

"So what are you planning?" Hayden asked impatiently. Drake could see her fists clenched and how tight the skin was around her eyes. The CIA agent was desperate to challenge the Blood King and Boudreau on their own playground.

"The one feasible option. We get close to the Stormbringer, get men aboard, and commandeer his ship."

Drake spoke quickly. "You can't just sail up in one of those USS Destroyers and threaten him? Make him surrender."

"That's the ideal scenario. But you're forgetting one important factor."

"They believe he may have both devices," Mai said softly. "In which case - he may set them off."

"He might anyway!" Ben exploded. "If he does in fact have them."

Drake shot him a loaded glance, but Ben just looked confused. The eighteen-year-old said: "You ok, Matt?"

Then, Hayden started laughing. "I get it," she bobbed her head, "I get it. You're offering the Blood King an olden day battle to make him believe it is a mark of respect. You're offering him to go down fighting like the pirates used to."

"You're going to board his ship?" Drake felt the adrenalin begin to flood through him.

"With an army," said Harrison grinning. "The USS Lake Erie has already sailed from Fort Lauderdale. This could be the biggest naval battle of modern times, against probably the greatest adversary since, well . . . Blackbeard."

Drake's elated expression said it all. "I have to get a bite of this. Can you get us onboard before they launch the strike?"

"Choppers are fuelled and waiting," Harrison said quickly looking at his watch. "The operation is still in planning, but even then it'll be touch and go."

Drake and Hayden were moving first. "We'll make it. Let's go."

CHAPTER THIRTY-FOUR

The Blood King stood alone in his primary stateroom. His gaze lingered around the walls and upon the images hung there: paintings and black-and-white photographs of Russia in its various forms; the revolution and the deposition of the Tsars; depictions of Petrograd in chaos; and Lenin. The Socialist state at the height of its power. The superpower years. Moscow. The new Russian Federation.

Good. Bad. It mattered not to the Blood King. Russia was his country. His home.

So, he thought, the Americans are coming. He had known it would happen since the day he made the conscious decision to end his lifelong quest. He hadn't planned on it happening so soon - the unearthing of Blackbeard's device had accelerated his schedule dramatically.

But no matter. Everything was in place, as it had been for years.

The ranch in Hawaii was almost fully populated. Two more to go. Boudreau had failed him yet again in that task. But Boudreau could yet prove useful. And when that maniac was dead or maimed or imprisoned . . . there was always the next.

In a few weeks we reach for the gates of hell, he thought. The prospect sent a barrage of icy chills through his body that not even the expectation of murder could match.

His eyes settled upon a thick file that lay open on the table. It contained the names, histories and a full information pack about each of the adversaries who had recently come to his attention. And once his attentions were aroused then Blood King did not hold back.

A heavy knife lay on top of the file, keeping it open. The non-smiling face of a soldier stared up from the page. A once soldier. Matt Drake. The other pages held information about every one of his cohorts and their families.

The lists were exhaustive, as required.

These were the people who had hunted him from the USS Port Royal to Key West; the people he had found and lost in that hotel in Miami.

The Blood King did not suffer such foolishness lightly.

The blood vendetta had been issued. On each of them and on every single member of their families. No future existed for them that wasn't filled with misery and torment.

The Blood King thought about his escape plan and the secure ranch in Hawaii. All was well. In the end, the ship was always going to be sacrificed and sacrificed hard.

He sat down to read the file again.

Justin Harrison and Jonathan Gates had done well.

CHAPTER THIRTY-FIVE

The USS Lake Erie ploughed the waters of the Bermuda Triangle, its four gas-turbine engines firing nine thousand tonnes of iron at thirty knots through the rich turquoise of the Caribbean. Its estimated time of arrival remained evenly at one hour from now.

Drake jumped off the chopper and immediately sought out the SEAL team's commander. There would be a lot of hierarchy involved with the troops. SEAL and Delta were more suited to his wavelength and more likely to let him integrate. Mai and Alicia tailed him. Hayden and Kinimaka sought the ship's captain, Hayden already on her cell-phone and no doubt requesting clearance.

Kennedy and Ben made a show of heading for the ship's galley, wanting no part in the testosterone-fuelled attack.

Twenty minutes later, with their places secured Drake, Mai and Alicia drifted towards the bow and the glorious panorama of glittering waters and electric blue skies that opened up before them. Drake stared for a while, taking it in, wondering how to phrase his next words.

"I don't think Wells died by a stray bullet."

The sentence hung and spun in the hot, dry air.

Mai's comment was soft, as soft as the caress Drake remembered. "He died because of his past, and the things he did. He died because he needed to die. Don't think you know his biggest secret, Drake. It would bring you to your knees."

Alicia remained uncharacteristically silent.

Drake trusted Mai with his life. He was shocked to hear her speak so. "I watched those soldiers' so-called interrogation in that village, Mai. I know Wells signed off on that. Don't tell me I don't know."

"If you think that's his most terrible secret, Drake, then you know nothing at all."

Drake felt a rush of anger. "Then enlighten me."

But there was silence. Drake considered the calibre of the two women standing next to him. Mai - one of the world's greatest agents bar none. Alicia - the most outspoken and confident woman he'd ever known, and one of the most deadly.

The fact that they were staring at the deck, not knowing what to say, sent icicles into his heart. For a moment he struggled for something to say. Then: "Alright, alright. But one day . . . one day you will tell me."

"One day," Mai whispered. "We will have to tell you."

He trusted Mai with his life, so he said no more. Instead he pointed towards the horizon. "Kick-off time's approaching."

A vessel snugged up against the skyline. A vast, gleaming-white Superyacht.

Alicia came to life, grinning like a hungry mountain lion who'd wandered into a busy shopping mall. "Let's get jiggy."

*****

A storm of helicopters darkened the Caribbean skies as the United States declared open war on the myth and the man they called the Blood King. The strategy had been dictated.

They were to exit the choppers using the FRIES system - a method where several soldiers descended a thick braided rope at the same time, one after the other, in a non-stop stream of manpower. Extra unmanned helicopters were present to provide covering fire. FRIES is a quicker alternative to abseiling, but more dangerous, as the descent is freefall. The strategists had deemed its use necessary for this mission. Fast-roping onto a ship takes one man less than thirty seconds and is used by the military when a rapid, massive build-up of personnel is needed.

"Fast-roping," Alicia licked her lips, looking insanely different now in army fatigues and safety-vest. "No matter which way you say it, it always sounds dirty."

Under fire, the helicopters closed in. Drake watched as the first few approached from the starboard side with bullets lacing the air around them. Now, a support chopper swept the ship's decks with lead, allowing the first chopper to swing down at a sharp angle. Rope-lines flickered into the air and unfurled towards the ship.

The chopper steadied. Men jumped out onto the ropes. The assault was on.

*****

Drake hit the deck and moved swiftly away, sensing rather than hearing Mai and Alicia landing and free-roping swiftly above him. He'd landed on the Helipad, glad to feel hard wood under his feet and running for the cover of one of the nearby tenders - a reasonable-sized boat used for ferrying people and goods to and from the mainland.

As he approached a head popped up from behind the prow. Drake double tapped without breaking stride and watched the man fall away. Another foe appeared from behind the tender. Drake fired again, sending him reeling against the ship's rail and his weapon flying overboard.

Mai and Alicia were now right behind him.

They skidded up to the base of the tender and surveyed the Lido - top - deck. The mishmash U.S. military force had already landed about thirty men on board, half at the bow and half at the stern, who were taking covering positions to help speed up the arrival of their fellow troops. The Blood King's men were stowed away in every available nook and cranny, being largely pinned down due to the excellent covering fire of the support choppers.

Drake pointed ahead to the double set of smoked-glass doors that led inside. "We need to get in to get down." He fired a shot that bounced off the heavy panes. "Thought so."

Mai shrugged. "It also means they can't fire out. Let's take a closer look."

Running in tandem, each covering the other, Drake led the two women towards the glass frontage. Three marines were already lurking to one side.

"We're blind here," one of them grated. "Can't see a thing through that shit."

"Blow it," Alicia said with a quick raise of her eyebrows.

There was a moment's thought, then one of the marines grinned. "Never refuse a lady," he said, glancing at the rest.

"You'd best stand back."

*****

Hayden and Kinimaka landed with a small force of men on the sun deck. As Hayden set foot on the sole - the decking - a bullet skimmed past the heel of her shoe. She pivoted quickly, firing from the hip. An enemy combatant with rope-like hair and a dirty face ducked and came immediately up to fire.

Kinimaka shot him as he descended. The heavy thump as he landed made even these heavy windows rattle. They were attached to a force of Delta men, all with Tweeters and hi-tech comms. Hayden heard a double-click in her ear - the signal to move forward - and then one of the soldiers took a shot to the arm.

Bullets zinged around them.

Three of the Blood King's men popped up from the vast gym that was the centrepiece of the sun deck and opened fire. Two were immediately gunned down, the quick reactions of the Delta team paying off. The third crawled behind a group of step-machines.

"No good," said Hayden pressing forward. "We have to get below. Boudreau will be below."

She fired a shot that skimmed the deck and made sparks fly from the well-greased machinery. Their assailant jerked his head up in shock.

A weapon barked.

Delta-one clicked three times, paused and then sent a double-click.

Enemy down. Move forward.

*****

Hayden stayed behind the Delta team with Kinimaka backing her up. They threaded the heavy metal of the gym and skirted the bubbling Jacuzzi. A man lay dead in there, face down. One of the Delta boys double-tapped him to be sure. His bubbling grunt of pain gave them an early warning of just how far these mercenaries were prepared to go for their megalomaniac boss.

Down a set of spiral stairs and they were facing an open doorway that led into the heart of the bridge deck. Once inside the Delta team fanned out, weapons held steady. A few of the Blood King's men lay dead on the inner carpet.

Hayden stared around a plush living room. A glistening wet bar held sway in one corner, holding an array of every kind of bottle she could imagine.

Through the inner door and they crept past a row of bedrooms, clearing them out as they went. A SEAL team had already been this way, but the Delta soldiers were leaving nothing to chance. Hayden darted glances from room to room. The decor was obscenely lavish.

Gunfire erupted above them. The Blood King's men, it seemed, were still buried away in some part of the upper cabins.

Beyond the guest cabins they came to the cinema. Hayden stared in amazement. Nineteen plush leather seats were arranged in rows around a wide cinema screen.

Kinimaka's jaw dropped. "Is this guy for real?"

"Forward," Hayden said. The sounds of combat now came from in front of them as well as above them. "Our men were murdered because this asshole wanted to make sure, Mano. Sure as your name means 'passionate lover' we're gonna get a slice of him."

"And Boudreau too." Kinimaka voice sizzled with hate.

"He's going out in chunks."

Beyond the cinema the oversize cabin area opened up into a circular room surrounded by glass windows. Even the ceiling was made of glass. The room's centrepiece was an enormous swirling Jacuzzi, surrounded by life-like palm trees and easy-chairs that even Kinimaka would drown in.

The sound of the bubbling Jacuzzi filled the small space. The group moved forward. A mini bar stood to one end of the room. A walk in cupboard at another. One of the Delta soldiers ran up the Jacuzzi steps to check it out . . .

. . . and fell back dead, clattering back down the pristine wooden treads, a ragged hole blasted through his forehead.

At the same time a hidden maintenance door burst open beneath the Jacuzzi and a stream of men almost tumbled out. Funny it might have been, if they weren't brandishing every kind of weapon from a serrated blade to a fully-automatic machine-gun.

And right before Hayden, bursting up from inside the Jacuzzi with water tumbling off him in torrents rose the lethal madman, Ed Boudreau.

His scream of blood-lust sent daggers through her heart.

CHAPTER THIRTY-SIX

Kennedy Moore stood on the deck of the USS Lake Erie, gazing across the rolling expanse of turquoise water that separated their ship from the Stormbringer. A stiff breeze took her long black hair and made it flicker around her face.

Ben was beside her. "Wow," he said, entranced for a moment. "You look like that woman from the movie - John Carter. The princess."

"Is that good?" Kennedy's thoughts were miles away.

Ben glanced around as if looking for Drake's back up. "I'll say," then he went quiet. "Missing him?"

"Huh? Yes, of course."

"Me too. And Hayden."

"They didn't have to go." Kennedy sounded angry.

"Hayden did. Boudreau murdered most of her men. Her friends."

"I guess so."

Ben's mobile rang. His attention diverted immediately and he turned away. "Karin? Hey, what's up?"

Kennedy took the few minutes of privacy to drift away. The last week or so, since leaving York, had flashed by in a blur. If she was being truly honest with herself the last year had flashed by in a blur. She felt the skin at the corner of her eyes tighten as she envisioned Kaleb yet again, the haunter of her dreams, as dead as he was ever going to be but still very much alive in her mind.

And in the minds of his victim's families.

A couple of them had kept in touch, probably through sympathy. Others hated her. The rest just didn't care. Maybe they had moved on.

She needed to move on. The death of Kaleb should have given her some closure. Instead it closed only one door, leaving many others ajar. Her brief time with Drake had eased those worries. There had even been times when she could forget. But recently, it seemed, the darkness behind the doors was calling, beckoning to her with blood-soaked fingers.

Ben ended his call. "Karin wants to help," he said with a worried look. "I've talked her out of it. For now."

Kennedy, regardless of her mental state, couldn't hide the sudden grin. "Just a small town girl . . . livin' in a lonely world . . ."

Ben glared and looked bemused, but then actually burst out laughing. "You old bastards and your Dinorock," he cackled. "I might actually give you that one."

"She took the midnight train . . ."

Kennedy heard footsteps approaching quickly. Harrison came into view. "The assaults heading down below decks at a fast rate. Shouldn't take too long now."

Kennedy knitted her brow. "You really believe that?"

She didn't see the men coming up behind Harrison. The men with their guns drawn.

CHAPTER THIRTY-SEVEN

Drake ran down another level to find himself facing a long corridor. A SEAL team were sweeping ahead, firing shots in quick bursts as they cleaned out each room. Drake quickly caught them up, Alicia and Mai close behind.

Stately bedrooms stood to left and right, lavish with gold and oak furnishings. A heavy burst of gunfire sounded ahead, and then two of the SEAL team went down. Drake filled the gap, kneeling and getting off two bursts into a throng of mercenaries who had just appeared ahead.

Behind him, Mai hit the floor, firing between legs. Alicia whistled in mock amazement.

Men were littering the floor up ahead and had stopped being replaced by others. The SEAL team leader saw two more of his own men go down and indicated a retreat into some of the state-bedrooms. Drake slipped in behind him, listening to his words as he thumbed his throat mic.

"Need more numbers down here. Think we've found Kovalenko. Repeat, think we've found Kovalenko."

*****

At that moment a grating voice rang out. "Stop! Stop firing!"

For a moment there was silence. The SEAL team shared a guarded look. Then, the same gravel-filled voice came again: "I am an honourable man! Lay down your weapons. Come fight me. Man to man."

A voice like that sent shivers down your spine. The SEAL team leader eyed Drake. "That the Blood King?"

Drake started, having drifted off for a second and wishing he'd said more of a goodbye to Kennedy. A quick hug and a peck and a "Laters," hardly constituted a loving departure.

He shrugged. "Think so."

"Throw your weapons down," the SEAL team leader said. "Lay flat on the ground."

"You know that will never happen, little American." The sneer in Kovalenko's voice was apparent. "I watch you even now. Yes, I watch you."

Drake cast about. Mai pointed to a little camera mounted above the far window. "Kovalenko likes to keep an eye on his guests."

"And you," the voice grew even more menacing, "you are Matt Drake. Mai Kitano. Alicia Myles. I have been informed of your little group," a breath, "... and it's attempts to undo me."

Drake swallowed heavily despite himself. This

didn't sound good.

"You try to thwart me at every turn. You think you beat me? In the end, it will do you no good, little man. I always win."

Alicia leaned in. "This prick knows too much."

"I know everything, Miss Myles. And that's another needle through your heart. My resources are very good and . . . very close."

Drake trusted everyone in their group with this, even Alicia, everyone except . . . there was one outsider.

"Are you thinking? Are you wracking your brains? No mind. I would not recommend that you survive this day. The rest of your life will be nothing but pain."

"You won't exactly be swanning around in luxury yourself, Blood King," Drake said a little awkwardly.

"Then let me say this. In return for your zealous explorations and in return for your eagerness to accept this mission to capture me I have issued a Blood Vendetta."

There was a pause. A terrible moment of heart-stopping dread.

" . . . on every member of your little team. And on every single member of their families. A bounty on all of you, I say! Now that comes straight from the Blood King's mouth. It has been broadcast through all my channels. The Blood Vendetta has begun."

Drake thought of Kovalenko's words. My resources are very close. And another comment slotted in alongside that one. Your eagerness to accept this mission.

How many people knew he'd wanted aboard?

He knew who the insider was. And that person was now taking care of both Ben and Kennedy on board the USS Lake Erie.

"NO!"

He leapt into the corridor, gun blazing.

*****

Kennedy Moore saw the mortal fear shining out of Harrison's eyes and knew her life was in deadly danger. All obsessive thoughts of Kaleb and his victims fled her mind a she half turned and saw sunlight glinting off the half-drawn weapons of three men coming up right behind Harrison.

Her world span. The Blood King could even reach them here?

No matter. She grabbed Harrison by the shoulders and hurled him towards them, screaming with all the breath in her lungs. Then she grabbed a shocked and sputtering Ben and ran for the nearest cover.

Thinking Damn it all, damn it all, why didn't I say a proper goodbye to Matt? What am I doing, putting all my compartmentalised shit before the love of this man?

There was no time. Harrison had stumbled among her foes, but they were military servicemen. They soon threw him off and gave chase. Her only chance was to let them fire and hope to God they missed. She had no weapon. Her only chance was to draw attention. Her constant screaming was causing soldiers and sailors to take notice and turn from the railings and their jobs.

The great gun turret stood before her. She ran headlong towards it and threw Ben to the floor a split second later.

The first shot rang out.

A bullet slammed between her shoulder blades.

She pitched forward, now seeing good men running towards her, shouting warning at her assailants. She saw Ben scooting around the enormous base of the turret and wished him luck and safety.

Saved, thank God.

She sensed the Blood King's men standing over her as her blood pooled on the deck.

Three more shots rang out.

She sensed no more.

CHAPTER THIRTY-EIGHT

Drake fired everything he had, sprinting headlong for the wall of the Blood King's men. Mai and Alicia backed him up without hesitation. Beyond the curve ahead they could hear the Blood King's manic laughter, a terrible beacon to guide them.

Drake closed in. The mercenaries who were still alive and kicking reached out to grapple him. The ex-SAS man didn't break stride. The terrible deadliness had taken over now, the man he used to be eclipsing the civilian as he thought about the Blood Vendetta and all it may mean.

His friends. Their families. All of them. Hunted by ruthless men without conscience, without souls.

Within three minutes he was through them, with no little help from Mai. Alicia mopped up the rear, and Drake just knew she'd be pissed at the relegation.

He hurdled one last man to reach the corner and peered around. The space to the right opened into a vast stateroom-cum-bedroom. The Blood King's abode.

The man himself stood to the left of the immense bed. Dmitry Kovalenko was a fit, broad man who seemed to be around forty. His face was sharply chiselled and showing the strains of running an empire whilst staying at myth status, but his demeanour radiated health and calm and superiority.

The harsh, rough voice that came out of his mouth belied his years. "You will never hold me. There is not a prison I could not own. A judge I could not control. A Government I do not already possess . . ." He left that statement hanging.

"I know something of your reach," said Drake, as his eyes examined every inch of the room, noticing nothing awry. "What I don't know is how you enforce it."

Kovalenko's weakness, it was becoming clear, was pure self-absorption. Maybe it came after a lifetime at sea with nothing to challenge him but the conundrum as to why celebrity jungle shows ever became popular.

"To own the man," Kovalenko grated, "you must own that to which he is most attached. That is all. You want to save this world? What kind of world is it you live in, that would make a monster like me?"

"How many men do you own?" Drake listened, but kept his surveillance up around the room. Mai and Alicia crept past on his left. The SEAL team backed him up. Kovalenko just stood there, arrogant and supreme.

What's he got up his sleeve?

"All of them," the Blood King said with an arrogant smirk, ". . . that matter."

"You have what each man loves," Mai said softly as she advanced lightly towards the bed. "By that, you mean his wife or child. You steal his heart and put him to work by threat and promise. That is what you do."

"My ranches, yes, are full of their little brats. Crawling with their women."

Drake spied the rusty device. It was behind the Blood King, partly shielded by his body, on an ornate sideboard.

Mai gave him a fleeting look, but her eyes said it all. Yes, I still have the device I spirited away from Hayden. Yes, I will keep it safe. And yes, I will not allow any one government to hold both devices at the same time.

It was the deal they had made between them. It was the only way they could work for a government and keep a healthy conscience. The Japanese had instructed Mai to claim both devices at any cost. The Americans, no doubt, wanted the same.

Drake and Mai maintained a different stance.

Kovalenko noticed their stares. "You kept the second device from me. Enjoy your victory. That is what sealed the Blood Vendetta around you."

Drake had had enough. "A curse I'll make you take back when I take you apart," he moved in quickly.

The Blood King barked out a laugh that wouldn't seem out of place if it came from a grizzly. "You lack vision, Matt Drake. Vision."

With that the Blood King flicked his wrist. Attached to the underside was a tiny black box that resembled a mobile phone. With another harsh flick he armed the device. His last words were directed at Drake: "You know she's dead already."

Then the ship started to explode.

*****

Ed Boudreau exploded from the water, a white shark wearing a crocodile smile. Time stood momentarily still for Hayden. Assailants were coming at her from the right, but Kinimaka and the Delta soldiers were picking them off.

Boudreau levelled his knife between her eyes and twirled the blade a little. "CIA agents are his favourite meal."

Hayden fumbled her gun up, but Boudreau leapt from the top of the jacuzzi and crashed down into her. His head smacked into her chin and she saw stars as she hit the floor.

Nevertheless, she scrambled back. Her vision still blurred, the knife point was her whole centre of balance. He could have killed her right then. The gun in his other hand was no doubt almost fully loaded.

But the manic glint in his eyes matched the glint of the blade and was just as deadly.

Two Delta soldiers now peeled off from the battle by the base of the jacuzzi and shouted at Boudreau to stand down. Without a moment's hesitation he shot one of them in the flak-jacket and leapt with amazing speed around Hayden.

His knife flicked out again, slicing a gash in her wrist, but now the fog was starting to clear and the pain of the wound actually helped. Hayden faced him down.

"You murdered them like a coward, Boudreau."

Now she leapt at him, straight at the blade. The surprise registered on his face just as she landed, took the vicious edges between both hands and jerked hard. The knife twisted so rapidly she heard one of the madman's wrists snap.

He grunted, and gritted his teeth. She flung the knife away and brought her head smashing into his nose, another piece of cartilage snapped. Still Boudreau only murmured, driving her fury on. She jabbed stiffened fingers towards his eyes, kicked out at his knees.

Boudreau blocked, but fell back, heading for the corner. The crazy arrogance never left his gaze. Kinimaka appeared at her shoulder.

"Put the gun down, asshole. You're done."

"Done?" Boudreau giggled as he flapped his broken wrist at them. "No. Not done. Just waiting."

*****

The Blood King's vessel, the Stormbringer, lurched in the sea, an aerodynamic behemoth brought to its knees. Explosions came from the hull around the bulkheads that made up the structural support.

Drake staggered along with the ship. When he looked up the Blood King was gone. Drake knew there was another level below this one, below the water line, some kind of maintenance level where the engines and machinery ran. He started forward,

255

wondering if there were some kind of trapdoor in the floor.

The SEAL team leader shouted to three of his men to retrieve the device from the sideboard: "No. This mission is over."

Drake turned black eyes on him. "Didn't you hear him? He's issued a vendetta. That means I can't keep them safe anymore. None of them."

The SEAL team leader turned away. "We go, . . . now." He signalled to his men.

"Kennedy," Drake muttered. "Ben."

Mai took his arm. "Quickest way to reach them is to get off this ship," she said, sounding as calm as if she was sunbathing on a Jamaican beach. "Save the Blood King for later."

"He'll get away."

The ship pitched dangerously forward, sending them all rolling towards the bed. A hole blasted through the floor to the starboard side, taking half the wall with it. A shocking flood of daylight burst through.

"We have to go. Now."

The roof collapsed at the far end.

"I saw Titanic," Drake muttered. "I know we have to leave before the ship starts to sink. But we have to get the vendetta lifted. This guy has the reach and capability to kill us all and everyone we love."

"I realise that," Mai whispered very softly. "I have family of my own."

Drake looked at her, suddenly worried.

"We can find the Blood King," Alicia said. "Better than anyone. You know that, Drake. Besides he has another agenda. Some lifelong-"

Another explosion and the entire boat listed in the water. Mai dragged Drake towards the hole in the hull, not taking 'no' for an answer. When Drake got to the hole he could see the USS Lake Erie floating in the distance and his mind was made up.

"Protect them now," he said. "Fight later."

They approached the ragged opening. As luck would have it there was no railing at this point. The blue Caribbean waited invitingly below where men were already swimming through the calm waters. The USS Lake Erie had launched Zodiac's to rescue them.

Drake jumped, Kennedy and Ben the sole focus of his mind.

*****

When the first explosion rocked the Blood King's ship Hayden and Kinimaka fell against each other. Boudreau recovered quickest. He'd been expecting it. He leapt at them, snarling, showing no signs of wanting to escape.

His eyes came down to stare into Hayden's, his nose touching her own. "You feel me?" He plunged the blade in the direction of her belly.

Hayden's world caught fire. Her lips touched Boudreau's in a grotesque parody of a kiss as she reeled forward in agony. But before Boudreau could twist the hilt and inflict more damage Kinimaka had rolled ungainly on top of him.

Boudreau wheezed as all the air left his body. The man was pinned, unable to move. Kinimaka took a few seconds to regain his equilibrium and then deliberately began to throttle him.

Hayden panted heavily. "Unconscious, Mano. Not dead."

The big Hawaiian turned puppy-dog eyes on her. "Are you-"

"Yes. He may . . . may have information about Kovalenko's next move," she groaned.

"You gonna live, boss?"

"Probably. Blade glanced off my jacket and went through my thigh. Hurts like a mother, though."

One of the Delta soldiers cried: "Zodiacs are outside. We need to evac! Now!"

Kinimaka scooped up Boudreau's unconscious body with one arm and Hayden with the other. "Just point the damn way."

CHAPTER THIRTY-NINE

Drake ran as if there was a fire at his heels. Somewhere along the climb to the top of the ship he lost Mai, but that was part of the plan. The Japanese woman would now use her resources to disappear, and the two devices would never meet again.

Drake felt a tug of sorrow, knowing that Mai and he might also never meet again. Once a mission was over, its avant-garde participants rarely assembled again.

And he was no Nick Fury. Or Joss Whedon, for that matter.

Sunlight flooded his eyes as he breached the top deck and came out onto the big mass of concrete. He shielded his eyes. Alicia was by his side. Hayden and Kinimaka were below, the CIA agent having being taken immediately to the sick bay.

Ben didn't even know his girlfriend was injured, but Drake wanted to be the first to assure him she was going to be alright.

He started towards the bow, but the area was deserted. "Could be anywhere, Drakey," Alicia said. "Just because the boy said 'meet me at the bow' doesn't mean he'll be allowed to stay there."

"Kid just wants to be DiCaprio for a minute, that's all." Drake was about to turn away when someone shouted above and behind him. He looked around to the next deck up, which began about half the length of the missile-cruiser.

There, standing at the rail was Ben Blake. There was blood on his hands, on his distraught face, and soaked through his shirt. Drake felt instant panic and a jolt of pure terror rocketed through his system.

"Kennedy!" He raced for the steps, leaping two, three at a time. "No!" He reached deck level and stopped.

Just stopped.

She was laid out on her back. A doctor stood next to her, head bowed. Half a dozen marines guarded her, but not from any further danger.

Kennedy Moore was dead.

Drake made it to her side before collapsing. At first he dared not touch her, but held his hands above her body, above her face.

Emotion took him like a storm, wracking his body, tearing into his soul.

"She saved my life," Ben said, and Drake squeezed his eyes shut so tight his head began to throb.

The woman he loved lay dead in his arms. She would never feel again. Never breathe again. All her thoughts and experiences and memories laid waste and scattered to the ethos. Nothing she worried about or cared about mattered anymore.

She was gone.

The Blood King had struck a hard first blow with his vendetta.

Drake looked up, straight at the sun, unable to see through the glare and the tears. The first person his gaze found a minute later was the man who had betrayed them all to the Blood King.

Justin Harrison.

Drake felt the rage explode. He flew at the man, screaming, wringing his neck between hands that shook with pain and rage and grief.

People tried to tear him away. Marines battered him with rifles.

They were a blur. An insignificance, a buzzing fly. Every ounce of Drake's hate poured into that stranglehold and nothing would tear him away.

Even minutes later, when Harrison lay almost dead and Ben's mournful voice finally registered to his ears.

"The Blood King took Harrison's daughter, Kate. He kidnapped her and made Harrison work for him. Oh, Matt."

And at last, one of the marine's blows caught him on the temple, sending him into a deep, crawling oblivion.

Drake collapsed to the deck and knew no more.

The End

The third book in the Matt Drake adventure
series will be available late 2012

I would love to hear from you! All genuine
comments welcome to:
davidleadbeater2011@hotmail.co.uk

Or – through Twitter:
@dleadbeater2011

Printed in Poland
by Amazon Fulfillment
Poland Sp. z o.o., Wrocław